The Return of the Mantra

Susie Williamson

Stairwell Books

Published by Stairwell Books
70 Barbara Drive
Norwalk
CT 06851 USA

161 Lowther Street
York, YO31 7LZ

www.stairwellbooks.co.uk
@stairwellbooks

ISBN: 978-1-939269-74-4

Printed and bound in the UK by Imprint Digital
Layout design: Alan Gillott

Front Cover: "Reed Flute Caves displaying the 'Crystal Palace of the
Dragon King' formations. Located in Guilin, Guangxi Province,
China" – DnDavis

Back Cover: "Sandstorm blowing through dead trees in Namibian
Desert" - Cheryl Ramalho

Dedication

Thank you to the team at Stairwell Books, who got behind the story and gave me feedback and space to produce a draft ready for publication. Special thanks to Rose Drew for her support in this project, and to the wonderful editorial assistants, Coral Hammond and Becca Miles, for their valued input and words of encouragement.

It has been a work in progress over many years, and during early drafts, when I was struggling to see it objectively, I sought the help of writer and editor, Debz Hobbs-Wyatt. She was instrumental in helping me to believe in myself as a writer who may one day be published.

I thank my family and friends for their support and encouragement: my mum who believed in me, and my dad who inspired in me a love and respect for wildlife, which would feature as a backdrop for the story. Lastly, Kate, my partner, who believed in me when I didn't, and who has lived through sleepless nights and the ups and downs of a debut novelist. Thank you.

Chapter 1

It was early, the skies filled with the golden colours of dawn, but already the river was bustling with life. Today was a special day.

I led the mule along the rise of the riverbank, wading through long reeds. It was hot, it was always hot on my homeland of Shendi: the drought had lasted all my fifteen years, and decades before. Despite the heat I pulled the hood down low over my face, as I passed women washing clothes, men fishing, and children swimming. Listening to their chat and laughter amidst a backdrop of squawking gulls, seeing the odd scowl cast in my direction, I felt like an unwelcomed stranger in my hometown. The hood was reassuring since it hid my face.

I felt something hit me on the back of the head, and then again. I rubbed my head, hearing giggles from behind, and turned to look. Two boys looked out from the reeds, one holding a handful of stones. Nearby, a man was watching from the river, water up to his waist, a young child sitting astride his shoulders. For a moment I thought the man might say something to the boys, but I wasn't surprised when he didn't. He glanced at me only briefly before turning away, lifting the child off his shoulders and swirling her in the cool water. My gaze lingered on the child as she reached out with chubby arms, pulling at her father's lips and nose, making gurgling sounds as she smiled at him. He smiled back and pulled her towards him, kissing her on the cheek before cradling her into his chest.

Out of the corner of my eye I saw another stone hurled in my direction. I stepped aside and pulled at the reins, hurrying the mule along. The closer I came to the estuary, the quieter the river. The townspeople were superstitious and feared the ocean. My mother, Mata, privately ridiculed rumours of sea monsters and evil spirits that pulled people deep into the ocean depths, to die a watery death. The shores of the estuary was one place I could guarantee to find solitude.

Further on beyond the crowds, a girl sat alone idly skimming stones. She glanced at me as I went to walk past, and to my surprise she smiled. I paused, looking back at her, and almost returned her smile. I felt suddenly awkward and turned away.

'Won't you sit with me?' she asked.

I looked back, confused. I had no friends my own age; Mata forbade it and besides, I had never had any offers. I thought it might be a trick, expected her to say something cruel, but her smile faded leaving a hurt look on her face.

I knew few people by name but I knew faces, and I was sure this was not a face I'd seen before. Dressed in a dowdy smock, she appeared poor like the beggars, but beggars never left the dark lanes and shadows of town. She looked to be a similar age to me; plain in appearance but with a subtle beauty in her dark brown skin and rosebud mouth. Feeling nervous and intrigued I dropped the rein, leaving the mule to graze, and climbed down the bank.

'I'm Ntombi,' she said, as I sat down beside her. She rolled a flat stone in her fingers, before flinging it out across the water. I watched it bounce four times across the surface before it sank. 'What's your name?' she asked, turning to face me.

'Suni,' I said, pushing the hood back from my eyes.

She nodded and looked back at the water. I did the same, nervously fiddling with my cape.

Finally she said, 'I don't remember seeing you at school.'

I felt my skin prickle and stared long and hard at the rippling water, wondering how to change the topic.

'I'm a weaver,' I said. 'I work at the market with mother.' I turned to face her. 'I haven't seen you before either.'

'I've got a job as well,' she said, leaning back to rest on her elbows. 'In the mornings, at the bakery. I just go to school in the afternoons.'

I was curious to know why she didn't go to school all day like other children, but I didn't go at all and kept my thoughts to myself.

We entered into an uncomfortable silence, broken by the sound of rustling in a nearby clump of reeds. A boy and girl emerged, faces flushed, hair ruffled. As the girl stopped to do up the buttons of her smock, the boy looked straight at me, frowning.

'What are you looking at?' he said, meeting my eye. He put his arm over the girl's shoulders and turned to lead her away. 'Witch,' he shouted back, a taunt I knew was meant for me.

I felt my cheeks burning and stared down into my lap. 'Witch' was a dangerous word.

I was surprised when Ntombi gently touched my arm and said, 'Ignore them.'

Still I couldn't look at her, and pulled the hood back down low over my eyes.

'I should go,' I said, standing up.

'Will I see you at the festival?' she asked.

I shrugged. I would be at the festival but I wouldn't be able to speak to her, not when my mother was there. I looked at her and smiled nervously, afraid of offending her after she'd been so kind.

She smiled back and said, 'Well if I don't see you before, come by the bakery tomorrow. I'll be there.'

I nodded and turned to climb back up the bank. All the way home I smiled to myself, daring to hope that I had found a friend.

Chapter 2

The King's annual festival was a day of celebration for loyal followers, which included virtually the whole town. Us few remaining non-believers kept our disloyalty secret. Still it didn't deter the gossip. As I passed families gathered in doorways readying to leave, the sight of mothers distracting young children from looking my way was a familiar one. I was Mata's daughter and that made me an outcast, a status I felt most strongly on festival days.

Turning the corner to home, I saw Mata standing on the doorstep, a look of impatience on her face.

'Where have you been?' she asked, as I approached.

'Just down at the river,' I said, tying the mule next to the trough.

'I wish you wouldn't wear that up,' she said, reaching for my hood as I walked past to go inside. 'You draw attention to yourself.'

'Stop fussing,' I said, shrugging her off as I walked over to the fireplace.

I kept my back to her as I looked down at the smouldering embers, wanting to hide my irritation. But I felt the tension between us and knew she was watching. With Mata there were always so many rules. I understood why, but sometimes they stifled. Moments passed and the silence stretched between us. I couldn't say I felt safer with the hood up, couldn't say I just wanted to be invisible. The last time I had told her of stones being thrown at me she had reminded me that our beliefs were bigger than any one of us, reassured me that we had each other, and hadn't let me go out alone for months. Back then we had argued. Once I told her I hated her. Never again. She had raised her hand as though about to slap me, but stopped. I had seen the tears well in her eyes before she turned to hide her face. I still remembered the sight of her shoulders shaking with silent sobs, still remembered the shame that I had felt at the thought I had made my mother cry, still remembered how her words had stung when she told me it was time I grew up. I was fifteen years old, almost sixteen, and had long vowed not to make her cry again. I was a young woman now and Mata was all I had.

'We need to tidy you up,' she said, breaking the silence.

She came up behind me and dragged a brush through my hair. I felt it pull but I didn't move. Festival days always left Mata flustered and ill-tempered. She moved round to stand in front of me and paused, tilting my head to face her.

'Why were you late?' she asked. 'Has something happened?'

I shook my head. 'Sorry.'

I could never tell her about Ntombi. I was taught to trust no one, especially a school goer which, aside from me, all children were. I was used to hiding my feelings from my mother, but this was my first big secret. Looking into her eyes I felt guilty, more so when she put her arms around me and hugged me into her chest.

'I wish we didn't have to go,' I said, knowing her mood would only worsen as the day wore on.

'You know we have to,' she said, standing back to face me. 'People will only talk if we're not there.'

I did know. She had raised me to know why we were different, how we stood for the truth while the rest of the town followed the King's lies. She was a believer of the old ways, a follower of tradition, and prayed to our true Great Spirit, the Mantra; a name not spoken in public. Compared to the strength of Mata's convictions, any troubles I faced paled into insignificance.

Making our way through the streets towards the market square, I felt paranoia set in. Like all festival days, the town guards were out in force; ordinary in appearance, aside from the clubs they carried. I had seen their brutality first-hand, when I witnessed a beggar boy, no more than five years old, beaten almost to death for stealing a handful of nuts from the market. It was a sight that had given me nightmares as my mind imagined the punishment for traitors.

I reached for Mata's hand and held it tight the rest of the way. Her pace was casual but I felt the tension in her arm. When we reached the square we saw the festivities were underway: people dressed in colourful costumes, juggling, stilt-walking, drumming and dancing. My mouth watered with the sweet smell of roasted nuts handed out by children with faces painted as fearsome lions. I watched as they veered away from us, and caught a glimpse of Ntombi in the crowd. When she caught my eye I looked away, pretending not to notice, and discreetly moved back behind Mata.

A sudden explosion of drumbeats signalled the King's arrival. A roar rose up throughout the adoring crowd, all eager to welcome their King. We were pushed back as the crowd parted to make way for the procession of palace guards: smartly dressed men wearing green tunics and belts holding knives strapped around their waists. Of all the guards these men held the highest rank; with duties to protect the King, theirs was the greatest honour. Their fearsome reputation preceded them; stories of these guards beheading men with just a single swipe of their blades were commonplace. With stony faces, expressionless, and cold glassy eyes, even the town guards were said to lack the courage to look a palace guard in the eye.

Mid-way through the procession, the royal sedan was carried on the shoulders of four palace guards. The crowd clapped and cheered at the sight of the King, sitting on a red cushioned seat studded with crystals, his face, as always, covered by a shroud. He was taken to a podium overlooking the stage, where he alighted and raised both arms at the crowd. As the people waved back, I looked around at the faces awash with tears. They believed they were in the presence of the divine; a man who never grew old; a man who still appeared youthful despite having lived for a hundred years or more; a man who kept his face covered, since any who looked into his eyes would be touched by a deathly power and turned to sand.

The King lowered his hands and the crowd fell silent. I turned to look towards the stage, and saw a mountainous scene revealed as the curtains parted.

The narrator, a boy, stepped onto the stage and said in a loud, clear voice:

'Our forebears were a primitive people, unknowing of the Earth Spirit Orag, Prince of Prosperity; the one true creator who guided us into the mountains to where the light of crystals shone deep beneath the earth. The tribes of old followed mere fables of the Mantra; lies that bound generations in ignorance and poverty, a lie that condemned innocent lives through the worship of mindless beasts.'

Actors wearing lion costumes came onto the stage, with clawed hands and feet, and wearing masks with fearsome red eyes and long fangs. They prowled around the set, growling and swiping the air, circling the tribespeople that arrived to offer prayers of worship to the Mantra. Every man, woman and child that came was mauled to death by the pride, but still more people came.

The narrator said, 'They blindly worshipped what would tear their flesh to pieces. But the Earth Spirit Orag took pity on their ignorance and delivered a messenger, King Rhonad, the Chosen One. Gifted to hear the Earth Spirit's words, Rhonad bravely ventured into the mountains to fight for our people.'

Rhonad's character came onto the scene brandishing a spear. The lions surrounded him, circling, manoeuvring to attack. Rhonad jumped up onto a boulder that led to a ledge hanging out over a cave. He had gained the higher ground, forcing the lions to split. The lions could only follow one by one, and Rhonad, skilled in spear fighting, fought each lion in turn. When the lions lay dead a curious breeze stirred, carrying a sound, a melody, a word, 'Orag'. Guided by the voice Rhonad jumped down from the ledge and entered the cave. Inside he saw the walls of the cave glistening with crystals.

Men arrived and on Rhonad's orders, fires were lit. The whole mountainside was set alight, burning trees and wildlife, turning once green slopes into a charred wasteland. Free from the threat of lions, and with the ground cleared, work began building the mines.

The final scene showed the market place, where crystals were traded for plentiful food, and extravagant wares brought by sea traders. The town of Shendi was founded, and the people came together to praise the new King.

The narrator concluded, 'And so came the Dawn of the New Age, when our mighty King, the Chosen One, overcame the tyranny of the mountain lions and opened the mines. Chosen to hear the Earth Spirit's message, to remain young when the world around him grows old so he can continue to deliver this message, the bravery of our great King has ensured our place as a respected port of trade, trade from which we all can prosper.'

There was a finale of celebratory drumming from all corners of the square. Actors and actresses re-entered the stage for a final bow, before turning to face the real King Rhonad. As they took to their knees, spreading their arms and kissing the ground, the crowd fell silent.

I looked among the tear stained faces as a prayer began to rise from the masses: 'Earth Spirit Orag, we thank you for the gift of prosperity you bestow upon us. Humble before you, we vow to serve your messenger with obedience and devotion. We pledge our allegiance, and the allegiance of our sons and daughters. Now and forever, we are your followers.'

Then silence fell as, in one sweeping wave, the entire audience fell to the ground in prayer.

Only Mata and I were left standing. Mata grabbed my hand and we fled before any had raised their head.

As we veered through the streets to home, Mata cursed through gritted teeth, 'Blasphemous lies!'

Chapter 3

'I swear it gets worse every time,' Mata said, once we were safely home. 'Damn fools, the entire town, every one of them kneeling at the King's feet.'

The prayer of worship to the Earth Spirit Orag was familiar, but it was the first time I had witnessed the entire crowd take to their knees and recite it. The image was firmly imprinted on my mind, along with a seed of doubt; how could the whole town be wrong? As though reading my mind, Mata placed her hands on my shoulders with a firm grip.

'It's the school, brainwashing generations,' she said. 'There's so few of us left. It's more important than ever that you stay close by me.'

I nodded. Loneliness gnawed my insides.

Her face softened into a sympathetic smile as she said, 'I know how lonely you are, Suni. I have friends now I can trust, but I had no one when I was your age.' She leaned forward and kissed me on the forehead. 'I'm sorry I was hard on you earlier; you know what I get like on festival days. I just worry. Tomorrow you turn sixteen, a young woman, and the time will come when you have to find your own way in life. You must promise me you'll always stay true to my teachings.'

I looked into her deep brown eyes, the eyes of a faithful believer of the Mantra, and saw my future. That I would follow her path had never been a question.

'I promise,' I said.

She held my gaze a moment before relaxing her grip and turning to the fireplace, laying the coals for tea. I took off my cape and slumped back on the bed, my shoulders tight.

My mother was all I had and I didn't doubt her, I couldn't; treated as outcasts by most of the town, we were all each other had. Besides, I didn't want to believe in an Earth Spirit and follow a King who would slaughter wildlife. Drought was all I had known; a desert, barren of wildlife. It hadn't always been that way. Mata told stories of life from before, stories I treasured. My childhood was filled with her magical tales: a land of thick forest, home to creatures I'd only seen in my imagination: big cats, boar, monkeys, birds, lizards… That was a time when the Mantra walked the earth, watched over by its guardians, the mountain lions: our true Great Spirit that wore the face of every creature. But after the King cleared the mountains, killing all wildlife, the Mantra left, deserting our land to drought.

I turned onto my side, hands clasped beneath my cheek, feeling the tension in my shoulders ease as I looked at the pillows. I was never too old for Mata's stories, and enjoyed hearing them most nights before sleep. It was my favourite time of day, the time when my mother was most relaxed. Together we would be cast away into tales of why the boar first grew tusks, or why the mountain lion exchanged a solitary life in favour of a pride. My favourites included tribespeople, hunters and gathers living in harmony with the land. Her imagination knew no bounds as she told of people with fantastical gifts: speaking with animals, controlling the winds, or seeing the future. Always she ended with a teasing smile, leaving me guessing fact from fiction.

The table was laid with bread and cheese, and a pot of mint tea.

We sat down, clasped our hands together, and said, 'Blessed be the return of the Mantra. Blessed be the return of the rains.'

It was a day Mata longed for, and a day I hoped to see; the Mantra return to our land and an end to the drought. But while Mata believed in the power of prayer, I wondered.

'Do you think the Mantra hears us?' I asked. Mata looked at me, one eyebrow raised. 'It's just, the festival; it seems *everyone* believes in Orag now.'

'The King is insane,' she said. 'Claims of an Earth Spirit are used to justify his madness.'

'But what about the shroud?' I asked. 'If Orag doesn't exist, where does the King's power come from, to turn people to sand just by looking at them?'

Everyone knew the story. Not long after the palace was built, some of the King's own men rebelled, tried to overthrow him and gain power for themselves. The spirit of Orag looked out through the King's eyes, and turned the bodies of the traitors to grains of sand. Followers praised the merciful King, who would forfeit his sight to protect loyal subjects from the Earth Spirit's power.

Mata reached across and squeezed my hand. 'This is why I don't let you go to school,' she said. 'Don't be fooled by the lies. There is no Earth Spirit. It's a lie told to keep the town afraid. Rhonad ruined this land, all for crystals. He lives in a palace three days trek into the desert, a place only the King and the palace guards can enter. He claims he is protected by Orag, with an enchantment that turns traitors to sand, an enchantment that protects the desert surrounding the palace; it keeps everyone away. No one goes near, not the town guards, not miners, not even pirates. It's all just nonsense to keep control of the crystals. You don't see ordinary people with crystals to trade, only guards.'

'But the whole town believes it,' I said.

'People fear the guards, they fear the King, and they fear a powerful Earth Spirit that no one can disprove. Generations are taught to feel shame for the old ways; they're taught to believe that life in this town now is civilized. There's nothing civilized by how the town came to be, nothing civilized about mocking your ancestry; tribespeople knew the value of humility, they knew their place among nature.' She cupped both hands around mine, and leaned forward. 'There is only one Great Spirit of this land and that is the Mantra; a spirit of nature that connects all that lives on the land and in the skies. It is our one true

11

creator and it deserted us because of the shame we brought. Now, its return is our only hope.'

'I know,' I said. 'I'm just saying, do you really think it could return? With so few people left praying to the Mantra, how can it hear us?'

She let go of my hands, leaned back in her chair and sighed.

'The older you get, the more you question me,' she said. She lowered her eyes, looking down at the table. 'You're starting to remind me of your father.'

I stared at her. It had been years since either of us had mentioned him. As a young child I'd asked about him many times. She would clench her jaw and turn away, but I would see the sadness in her eyes. 'You have no father,' was all she would say. I had assumed he was dead, and eventually stopped asking. And now, I reminded her of him, but she said that as though it was a bad thing.

Her hands were clasped together so tight the skin had turned white. I looked at her face; her light brown skin and the soft curve of her jaw contrasted with my own dark skin and square jaw.

'Will you tell me about him?' I asked. 'Did he die?'

She looked up to meet my gaze and said, 'No, he didn't die. It would have been easier if he had. He chose a life at the mines over his own family. He left when I was heavily pregnant with you, and never came back.'

I couldn't speak, couldn't move. Everything I had imagined about my father was shattered: a kind man, loyal to his family; a father who would have played with me, taught me to fish, let me ride on his broad shoulders. But he was none of those things. My own father, working for the King, the man Mata spent her life working against. It hardly seemed possible.

'Why didn't you tell me?' I asked.

'Because I hoped not talking about it would mean you wouldn't question the path I've laid for you. You look so much like him. But I tell you now, your father works for the enemy, and that makes him *our* enemy.' She reached for my hand. 'Loyalty to the Mantra, resisting the King's lies, it takes sacrifice. Your father was a weak man. You must be strong. We're surrounded by bad influences, people who would turn

12

you against me. You must be sure of yourself, and know that you're *my* daughter.'

Her expression was stoic; a look I knew well: a woman with devout beliefs. It was hard to imagine how she could have loved a man who didn't share the strength of her convictions. And she had loved him. I saw the pain she carried behind the poise.

'But why did he leave?' I asked. 'Why go to work for the King?'

'Because he didn't understand as I did: there are those loyal to the Mantra, and those loyal to the King. There can be no in-between, no compromise. Fazi, your father, wouldn't have it. He said I should accept the world was changing, accept that our resistance was too weak to stand against the King's regime. He said the way to change things was to join forces, change things from within, to spread the word of the Mantra among those in danger of forgetting entirely. He was wrong. The enemy have no interest in the truth of the Mantra.'

'You haven't seen him again?'

'No,' she said. 'And I don't want to. Your father is in the past. You must believe that.'

I nodded, and swallowed the ball of tears welling in my throat. He had abandoned us, abandoned me, but my mother had not. She had always been there, and always would. *You never left me.* I *was* her daughter. I saw it now, all the times she had demanded answers, suspicious, wondering whether I would betray her. I would never betray her again.

'Say it,' she said.

I looked her square in the eye and said, 'He's in the past.'

'I know it must be hard for you to hear,' she said, 'but now you're coming-of-age, it's time you knew the truth.' Her gaze drifted to the flickering candlelight, seeming to look into a faraway place.

'Mata?'

Still staring into the flame, she said, 'In the days of the Mantra there were those gifted in windfinding, dreamwalking, speaking with the animals, and there were some who saw the world without time.'

'But they're just stories,' I said.

Her eyes flicked back to look at me with a penetrating gaze.

13

'No, Suni. My ancestors, *your* ancestors, they were gifted people. I think remnants of the gifts remain.'

'What do you mean?' I asked.

'Every night, for the past year, I've had the same dream. It's confusing, just flashes of images, but I see your face in a dark place, your eyes looking down into a light in your hands. You look different: creases around your eyes, older. I think it's the future.'

'You're a seer?'

'I think there are traces of the gifts still in our blood, but in me it's weak. But you...'

'Me? I haven't seen anything.'

'I think you have a gift not yet realised. In the dream, the light you're holding, it's no ordinary light. At first it's small, like a candle, but the more you look into it, it grows. I don't see what you see, but I feel it.'

'Feel what?'

'Hope.'

I looked at her blankly.

She leaned forward in her chair and said, 'I think my dream is telling me that you have a part to play in the Mantra's return. The Mantra may have left but it is all seeing. As long as there are those of us staying true to our traditions, remembering the Mantra as our true Great Spirit, a spirit that wears the face of every creature that ever lived, then there's always hope. And now, in you, I believe hope of the Mantra's return has never been greater. Your destiny is so much greater than mine. You *must* stay on the path I've set before you. *You* are all of our hopes.'

Her eyes glowed. I felt her unwavering belief as she gently squeezed my arm. Perhaps she had glimpsed something extraordinary, but if it was true, what light, what dark place was I destined to find? She spoke as though her lifelong commitment to the old ways had all been for this, but for what? I was just an ordinary girl, who saw nothing other than the world around me. I looked at her, wanting to believe, wanting to live up to her expectations, wanting to feel close to the only person I had, but I was left with only doubt.

14

She stood up from the table and said, 'One day you'll realise how special you are.' She reached for my hand to follow. 'Come, I've got something for you.'

Chapter 4

We lived on the northern edge of town. From the outside our house looked like any other, a sandstone cottage with a grass roof covering the single room. Inside, hanging on the rear wall, a tapestry concealed steps down into the cellar; this hidden room, Mata's workshop, was known only to Mata's closest allies. In the cellar, Mata prepared ointments, poultices and potions, and taught me all she knew. The practise of herbal lore was a remnant from our distant past, which, under the King's law, was now considered an act of treason.

She led the way down the steps, and opened up a wooden chest in the corner of the cellar.

'I've got a birthday present for you,' she said, taking out a roll of old cloth and handing it to me. 'It's been my most treasured possession. Now it's yours.'

In the dim light, I carefully unrolled the cloth, threadbare in places, and saw, painted in faded ink, a picture of a mountain lion lounging in the sun. Intricate brush strokes brought to life the slender, muscular body, eyes underlined with tear-shaped markings, and black tufts of hair tipping its tail and ears.

'It was painted by my grandmother,' she said. 'I named you Suni after her.'

I looked at my mother with wide eyes; she'd never spoken of family before.

'It was the only heirloom I could salvage,' she said. 'I never met my grandmother, but my mother told me about her, how every year she went on a pilgrimage to the mountains. She was a seer, and joined the resistance, fighting the King's men in the mountains.' She paused, then continued. 'No one in the resistance survived.'

I stared into the picture, feeling unworthy of such a treasure. Mata spoke of *our* bloodline, but it was Mata who was gifted, a seer like her grandmother. She had said it herself; *I* looked like my father. I had no extraordinary view of the world. I wasn't brave like Mata or her grandmother; a woman who had died for her beliefs, for my future. In that moment, all we had lost hit me. I knew the old stories of the Mantra living in a distant forest beyond the mountains, the sacred forest; the lions were its guardians, protectors of the gateway. But it had always felt too long ago to feel real. Now, hearing what my great grandmother had sacrificed, to think of the sacred forest gone, the mountains swarming with guards and miners, was devastating.

I looked at Mata, as though seeing her for the first time, and asked, 'What about your parents? What happened to them?' I only knew that Mata had been raised by Faru, an old man, unrelated.

She took my hand, guiding me to sit beside her on the bench, and said, 'The town was still being built when I was born; people lived in villages led by tribal leaders. The tribes held out for long enough, but raids by the King's men grew more violent. They demanded allegiance to the King. Any who refused were denounced as witches and burned at the stake. It's what happened to my parents.'

'You saw that!' I said.

'I was ten years old. A neighbour hid me, smuggled me into town, and gave me to Faru to raise as his own.'

I couldn't imagine it, didn't want to imagine it; I'd never realised the risks were so high.

'They don't still kill people now, do they?' I asked, frightened by the thought I had been called a witch just that morning.

She shook her head and said. 'It's not like the old days when belief of the Mantra was widespread. There are so few of us left now. The regime don't fear an uprising, because they know there's not enough of us to rise up.'

Feeling the brittle painted canvas in my fingers, I said, 'But this is our history. How can people just forget?'

'If you live a lie for long enough, it's easy to forget the truth.' Mata looked away. 'In the beginning people feared for their lives; over time they were seduced by the idea of wealth. It's only the King and his men who profit from the mines, but who would dare to challenge them, a regime protected by an Earth Spirit with powers to turn you to sand?' She looked at me. 'The fact his rule is based on lies, is surely the reason why he keeps such tight control of everything: the lessons taught at school, the books people read, even the time we shut our doors at night. People haven't had to think for themselves for so long, I fear they've forgotten how to. But I'll tell you something.' She leaned closer and lowered her voice. 'For all the fear the King's created, I think he's more afraid than anyone.'

'What do you mean?'

'Rhonad denies the existence of the Mantra, and he knows that's his biggest lie; he knows the Mantra's power better than anyone. The day he killed a lion with his own hands was the day he felt that power; he hasn't aged since. It's why he outlaws all ties with our history, to guard against the Mantra's return.'

She reached up to brush a loose lock of hair from my face and said, 'Praying to the Mantra, remembering our history, keeping knowledge alive, that's how we stay connected to the Great Spirit; that's how we defy the King.'

She stood up and scooped her long, dark hair into a scarf. I watched her browse the shelves, selecting woodvine leaves, sesame oil and dates. I recognised the ingredients; a poultice for arthritis, most likely for Faru. While she set to work lighting the coals, I took a book I was studying from the shelf; a catalogue of herbal remedies written by Mata.

I'd committed most of the book to memory, except words of the old tongue. Mata's knowledge of the old tongue was limited, but wherever she could she had named plants, trees, fungus and flowers with their true names. The breathy syllables and clicks formed words I could write but struggled to pronounce. Mata described it as a language formed from the breath of nature, words from the beginning, first spoken by the Mantra. In her stories of gifted people, some, like

18

windfinders, were born with knowledge of these powerful words, able to string them together into spells. I looked up from the book, watching Mata dry leaves over the fire. 'Where did you learn words of the old tongue?' I asked.

'From my mother,' she said.

'You didn't just know them?'

She dropped the charred leaves into a wooden bowl, grinding them together with the oil and dates before she replied. 'Only those with gifts connected to nature are born with knowledge of the old tongue: people gifted to control the winds, or speak with animals... In any case, like I said, my gift is weak.'

I tried to imagine someone changing the course of winds, or speaking with a cat or a mule, or seeing the future... I looked at Mata, sceptical, wondering just how much she would be willing to believe in the name of the Mantra.

She scooped the poultice into a jar and screwed the lid down tight.

'I'm done here,' she said, looking at me. 'Do you want to come with me tonight?'

Some evenings Mata went up to the fields under cover of dark, gathering specimens for her potions. I'd always thought it sounded exciting and had asked many times if I could go with her, but she'd never let me. Finally she was offering, I wasn't sure I wanted to. Only farmworkers were allowed in the fields; for market traders like us, it was strictly out of bounds. Even walking the streets after curfew felt too risky after hearing about people burned at the stake.

'What about the curfew?' I asked. 'What if the guards catch us?'

'They won't. These days the night patrol don't bother with the streets or the fields; come dusk they're all at the river, drinking. Besides, I go prepared.'

She dressed in a cape with two pockets hidden in the lining, one to store any specimens she found, the other to hide a flask of homebrew: guards' taste for liquor apparently made them easy to bribe. Upstairs she picked up a sack, used for collecting reeds; she'd always said it was the perfect excuse for being in the fields. I looked up at the rafters, bulging with more reeds than we could ever weave. I'd never doubted her reasoning before, never doubted she could keep herself safe even though I knew gathering reeds was only permitted at the riverbank.

'Well,' she said, opening the door ajar. 'Are you coming?'

I hesitated, before grabbing my cape and following Mata out into the night.

Chapter 5

Curfew was upon us. Our neighbours – field workers, fishermen and market traders – were safely indoors or heading that way. Still, I pulled up my head. Except for the scratching and howling of scavenging cats and dogs, the streets were quiet.

Faru was sitting outside his house, in a creaking old rocking chair, smoking his pipe. Usually he was pleased to see us, but tonight he looked worried.

'What are you doing here at this time?' he said, his voice a gruff whisper. He got up from the chair and jostled us inside, closing the door behind us.

'For goodness sake, Faru,' Mata said. 'What's wrong with you? There aren't any guards around.'

'You push your luck,' he said to her. 'And now you're bringing Suni out after curfew!'

'What's your problem?' she said. 'You know as well as I do, guards don't patrol the streets at night. They've got the townspeople so well trained, they don't have to.'

He looked down at the sack under her arm. 'You're taking your daughter to the fields?'

'She has to learn some time,' Mata said. 'And before you say it, we'll see no guards. They're all drunk on the riverbank at night these days.'

'A sack of reeds won't help you if you do see a guard,' he said.

'Mata?' I said, reaching for my mother's arm.

She turned to me and said, 'Faru just worries. It's ages since I last saw a guard up there. When he asked what I was doing in the fields, I showed him a sack full of reeds. I told him I'd not had chance to get out in the day, told him I'd come to the fields because I didn't want to intrude on the guards' camp at night, told him it wouldn't happen again. I didn't even have to bribe him with the wine.'

Faru was shaking his head. 'Times are changing. It's not safe. I hear things: deals made with guards; neighbours spying on each other.'

'I don't believe that!' Mata said. 'And even if they have heard rumours, guards aren't worried about us; they don't see a handful of people dealing in medicines as a threat.'

'How can you be so bloody-minded, after what happened to your parents?'

'That was a long time ago,' she said.

'Maybe so,' Faru said, 'But with Suni still not going to school, people talk.'

'Let them talk,' Mata said.

'Whatever you're trying to prove, don't involve your daughter.'

He reached for my shoulder but I stood firm, linking my arm through Mata's. I was afraid to go and wanted to stay, but I wouldn't stand against my mother; I couldn't. Locked in a stare, they fell silent. I looked from one to the other. Faru was family; I'd never heard them argue before.

'We've brought your poultice, Faru,' I said, eager to ease the tension.

Mata took it out of her pocket and held it out to him.

'Take it,' she said. 'You won't be much of a carver if your hands seize up.'

Reluctantly he took the jar.

Mata put her hands on my shoulders and turned me around, leading me back to the door.

'Don't worry,' she said, glancing back at Faru. 'We'll be fine.'

As we stepped out into the street, I turned to see Faru keeping a watchful eye on neighbouring windows.

Dark corners of the market square stirred with the sounds of shuffling feet, muffled voices and a baby's cry. The smell of ale was unmistakable, as were the pairs of eyes watching our every step. These beggars, once members of respected mining families, had been made official outcasts after being caught smuggling crystals from the mines. Now their only potential employment was as water-carriers, tasked with watering the farms. For their labour they were paid a pittance, most commonly spent on liquor to forget the drudgery of their lives. Most respected townspeople kept a distance from their ragged clothes and stale odour, with only a few, like Mata, taking pity on their unfortunate offspring with offerings of bread and cheese. But tonight, aware of our vulnerability in the lonely shadows, she kept a safe distance.

We turned out of the square into a narrow lane, and were soon immersed in dark alleyways that wove around big storage buildings used for the market. It was unfamiliar territory to me and I clutched Mata's hand, as she navigated through the lanes that eventually merged into wide tree-lined avenues. The only trees I had seen before that night were the few that grew along the riverbank. This was a rich neighbourhood: the large one and two storey houses, with their own private courtyards were a stark contrast to the humble dwellings I was used to.

'Town guards and miners own these houses,' Mata whispered. 'Not difficult to see who benefits from the crystal trade, is it?'

I shook my head and tightened my grip on her hand, feeling my palms sweating: I hadn't expected to be walking straight through the guards' neighbourhood!

'Don't worry,' she said. 'There's never anyone about at this time of night.'

Still I quickened my pace, and was glad she kept to the cover of trees.

The further south we went, the bigger the houses, with torch lit gardens showing off extravagant flowers and shrubs. Gradually the landscape opened out into sprawling farmland cultivated with maize, okra, beans… I could never have imagined so much vegetation, like an oasis in the desert. I inhaled the fresh smells as we slipped down narrow dirt tracks separating the fields. But the deeper we went, I realised that without the back-breaking efforts of water carriers, the crops would fail: the man-made tributaries bordering the fields appeared an inadequate irrigation system for land so arid.

Mata waded through a clump of reeds growing in a shallow tributary, and scoured the ground bordering a field of maize with bird-like precision. I waited in the lane, listening, nervously clenching my fists as I looked up and down the track. After a moment of quiet I started pulling reeds. My hands were soon sore and bloodied from the effort.

Mata returned to show me the ragweed and red caps she'd found. While explaining that they're often found growing alongside each other, something caught her eye in the reeds. She reached in, and began picking berries from a lone sorral bush.

I stopped, rigid, hearing footsteps. Mata hadn't looked up from gathering berries.

'Someone's coming,' I whispered.

She paused, listening. The footsteps were getting closer, accompanied by a swishing sound like crop being beaten. She grabbed my hand and pulled me into the long maize, pressing me flat into the dirt as she lay on top of me. I peered up over the edge of the narrow rut, a sickly feeling in my stomach to see we had left the sack behind. It was out of reach and too late to go back for; the footsteps were almost upon us. A group of men stopped just feet away from our hiding place.

'What's this?' one man said, kicking the sack.

'Told you I heard something,' another said. 'They're out here somewhere. I had a tip-off in town.'

The group dispersed, some investigating further down the lane, others swinging wooden clubs into the maize close to where we hid.

I shut my eyes tight, barely daring to breathe as I heard them say, 'Bloody witches, they're like vermin.'

After a long, thorough search they finally moved on, but it was a while before Mata moved.

Finally she whispered, 'We'd better get back.'

We stole back through the fields like fugitives. Even when back in our part of town, I didn't feel safe. Faru had been right, someone was spying on us; by the time we reached home I was still shivering with fright. I tried to untie my cape but my fingers were numb. Mata rubbed my hands in hers until feeling returned.

'Better?' she said.

I looked at her wide-eyed.

She cupped my face in her hands and said, 'Don't worry, they didn't see us. I'll do some digging, find out what's going on. It'll blow over.'

But not even a cup of hot sugary tea could reassure my fears.

Lying in bed that night, I joined Mata in prayer: 'Blessed be the return of the Mantra. Blessed be the return of the rains.'

I tried hard to focus on the words, but instead found myself listening out for the sound of unwelcome footsteps.

Chapter 6

I woke with a start before dawn, feeling my nightgown damp with sweat. I didn't dare close my eyes again, afraid of the nightmare: running through dark alleyways, hunted by a mob of people I knew. Trapped in a dead end, a figure was waiting for me there: shrouded in a long black cloak, it had no face, just the depths of dark despair.

'Oraaag,' it had spoken in a low growling voice.

I sought solace in prayer, whispering the words over and over: 'Blessed be the return of the Mantra. Blessed be the return of the rains.'

Mata was still sleeping. For a while I watched the gentle rise and fall of her chest, until, restless, I crept slowly out of bed, taking care not to wake her.

The sky transformed into mauve as the sun peeked over the rooftops, but even first light could not ease my anxiety. I tiptoed around the room, making a start on the morning routine. Most days I rushed through the tasks without particular concern, but that morning I was intent on taking my time, attentive to the rituals and finding comfort in familiarity. Once washed and dressed and with mint tea brewing by the fire, I set about organising our wares for market: mats, baskets and bowls all woven from grass; and Mata's tapestry. Now the festival was over the market would be busy.

Mata woke to find me heaving her cumbersome loom up onto the cart.

'What are you doing?' she asked, grabbing the frame I was struggling to balance. 'You'll hurt yourself.'

'I've got it,' I said, but stopped upon seeing her look of gentle warning.

Mata secured the load before ushering me back into the house, where she sat me at the table. I looked down into my lap, avoiding her eye as she sat down across from me.

'How long have you been up?' she asked.

'A while,' I said.

She reached across, tilting my chin to face her, and asked, 'Couldn't you sleep?'

I didn't want to tell her I was afraid she was going down a path I was too scared to follow. But I was afraid.

'You won't go back to the fields, will you?' I asked.

She let go of my chin and looked down at the table. After a moment she looked back at me, a soft smile on her lips.

'Not for a while,' she said. She reached up, gently brushing a finger through my hair. 'I think Faru was right. I'm sorry; I shouldn't have taken you.'

The trust she had shown me the night before was gone. She was strong and brave, but I wasn't. And now she saw it. Seeing her posture reserved and guarded as she poured tea and sliced the bread, I felt ashamed. Throughout breakfast she kept the conversation firmly on the day ahead at market, and I knew I had failed her.

On the way to market I saw the elusive greetings Mata shared with acquaintances, and wondered who else saw the discreet nods and sly handshakes. I thought over Faru's warning, of neighbours spying on each other; someone had told the guards where to find us last night. Was that someone watching now?

I focused on our trusty mule as she pulled the cart into the market square, already bustling with merchants setting up for the day. Once the cart was unloaded and our wares laid out, I left Mata to catch the early morning sales, and set off with the mule for our routine walk to the river. Out of Mata's sight, I pulled up my hood. I stopped at the junction, undecided: straight on to the river or left to the bakery? I headed straight on: now more than ever, forging a friendship with

Ntombi felt like betrayal, and besides, I was eager to get away from the crowds.

I kept my hood pulled low and headed upriver, keeping my eyes fixed ahead as I passed people going about their morning chores. Further on, on the quiet shores of the estuary, I stopped to let the mule graze in the reeds while I gazed out over the ocean, intrigued by its limitless expanse and constant ebb and flow. Surrounded by uninhabitable desert, sea-faring merchants were the only reminder of a world beyond the confines of our town.

Canoes were heading for shore. Sea traders were a common sight at market: wealthy merchants and pirates alike were welcomed by the town guards, who had no scruples when dealing in crystals. Those who sold ordinary goods, like Mata, bartered with the raft people. They arrived at our shores only in the summer months, visits I looked forward to. Mata's old friend, Nisrin, was of the rafts; I loved to hear her fascinating tales of life at sea.

I pressed a hand to my eyes to block the sun's glare and squinted hopefully out towards the horizon. As I hoped, the rafts were anchored: a floating community, home to a hundred or more had arrived. A smile spread across my face as I picked up the reins and led the mule back to market to tell Mata the news.

The market was bustling with familiar sights and sounds: the commotion of raised voices haggling over goods; the rattle and shake of coffee beans tossed as they roasted; the rush of dried mung beans poured into great vats of water to cook; the huge bowls of richly-coloured, aromatic spices. Seeing people go about their business as though it was just another day, I pulled my hood back, leading the mule to the trough where I secured her reins.

Mata was at the stall, busy at her loom, surrounded by piles of baskets and rolls of grass mats. When I told her the rafts had arrived, she smiled, but only half-heartedly. I spotted her fleeting glance to the empty plot where Sisile was usually selling shawls.

'Where's Sisile? I asked.

Mata shrugged, not meeting my eye as she said, 'She must be sick. I'll call round later, see if she needs anything.'

She was hiding something; I could tell by the uncertain tone of her voice, and the way she stared, concentrating on the warp, even though I knew she could work the thread with her eyes closed. Sisile was skilled in herbal lore, one of the few people Mata trusted.

'Make a start,' she said, still not looking up. 'Three mats have sold already.'

Weaving grass mats was my job and, being of practical value, they sold well. Mata's loom with the comb, reed and needle was something I still couldn't fathom. The traditional designs of her tapestries had stood the test of time, and were particularly popular with the rafts.

Over, under, over again with the reeds; focus on repetitive motions provided distraction from my worries. By mid-morning Nisrin had arrived and headed straight for our stall. She was always a welcome sight, none more so than today. I looked upon her weather-beaten face and wide smile, smelt fresh sea air in her thick blond hair as she hugged me. She turned to Mata and planted a kiss on her mouth, her hand lingering on Mata's cheek before she turned back to me, holding out her hand. As always, I gently smacked her closed hand and she opened it to reveal a gift.

'It's a pearl oyster,' she said. 'Look inside.'

I levered open the two halves and found inside a perfectly smooth, iridescent stone.

'How's life at sea?' Mata asked, emphasising each word.

Nisrin gently frowned at Mata, curious, as I was, by the casual question at odds with her tone of voice.

'What's up?' Nisrin asked.

Mata smiled weakly.

Nisrin looked at me and then back at Mata.

'Dear friend,' she said to Mata. 'Don't tell me you're finally ready to run away to sea?' She ended with an amused smile and a confused frown.

Mata turned to me and in a controlled voice said, 'Suni, go and get us some coffee, will you?'

Nisrin didn't drink coffee. I looked from one to the other, wanting to stay but knew I was being excluded. I glanced across at Sisile's empty plot but Mata would give nothing away. I was sixteen years old but was being treated like a child; I had no one to blame but myself. I left them whispering together, and headed towards an old woman roasting coffee beans over a pile of white-hot coals. I focused my gaze on her gnarled, callused hands as she swirled the coffee pot, seemingly oblivious to the fiery heat that blackened her fingertips. Watching her pour two mugs of coffee, my thoughts drifted. When I handed the old woman a coin, watched her bite down on it with the few teeth she had left, my decision was made; I would look for Ntombi. After all, I too needed a friend.

Chapter 7

Mata and Nisrin had paid little attention to my excuses for leaving the stall. Nursing my bruised feelings, I veered out of the market in the direction of the bakery.

Turning the corner I saw Ntombi appear from a side alley, her smock covered in flour, pushing a wheelbarrow laden with stone.

'I thought you weren't coming,' she said. 'I've just finished.'

I smiled, hoping she would smile back, but she appeared flustered.

'Sorry,' I said. 'I was busy at market.'

'I saw you at the festival, yesterday,' she said.

I felt my cheeks flush and tried to hide it with a shrug.

'I didn't see you,' I said.

She put the barrow down and rubbed the small of her back.

'Well, come by tomorrow,' she said. 'I'll be here.'

She took hold of the handles and lifted the barrow.

'Wait,' I said, desperate for her not to leave. 'Why's the baker getting you to move that?'

'It's mine,' she said. 'He pays me in stone so I can finish my house.'

'You've got to take that home? But it's too heavy. I could help you carry it.'

I stepped forward, but stopped when she didn't move aside. My offer seemed to make her uncomfortable; I thought she might refuse.

'Really, I don't mind,' I said.

She shrugged her shoulders and let go of one of the handles, stepping aside so I could move in beside her.

As we set off down the lane, awkwardly pushing the barrow between us, I was confused by her silence; she had been so friendly the day before. At the end of the lane, she went straight on, away from town towards the river.

'Where are we going?' I asked.

'It's this way,' she said.

We crossed the bridge over the river, and headed out across barren wasteland, where I saw a lone shack in the distance. The silence between us felt awkward, but I didn't know how to fill it; closing in upon her home, I realised just how poor and isolated she was. The shack appeared little more than a ruin, with holes littering the rough walls, and a grass roof crudely assembled; this amateur building would give little shelter in a sandstorm.

Something broke the quiet, coming from inside the shack: it sounded like pots smashing and scuttling feet.

'Damn dogs,' Ntombi said, putting down the barrow. She picked up a stone in each hand and ran on, yelling, 'Get out of here!'

A dog appeared in the doorway, growling and baring its teeth. Ntombi threw the first stone wide and the dog stood its ground, barking. When the second stone caught the side of its leg, it yelped and fled.

Ntombi came back for the stone and said, 'I can take it from here.'

Seeing her flustered, I stood aside and watched her lift the barrow. She started to push it, but paused and looked back at me.

'I haven't got much,' she said, 'but you can come in, if you want to.'

I nodded and smiled, following her the rest of the way.

Ntombi tipped the stone into a pile at the side of the shack, and then led the way inside. There was little in the way of homely comforts, just a table and stool, a makeshift fireplace, and a pile of blankets I assumed served as a bed. I couldn't imagine anyone living here, and was about to ask if she lived alone, when I saw someone nestled in the blankets: a small child, about two years old. On the floor next to him was a cup of water and an upturned bowl, with porridge spilt on the floor. It felt desperate, a child left alone in the wilderness, defenceless against scavenging dogs. I expected Ntombi to go to him, but she just glanced at him briefly before taking a brush and sweeping shards of broken pot into a pile.

'Is he alright?' I asked, kneeling down next to the boy, wondering how long he'd been left alone.

'His name's Wanda,' Ntombi said. 'He's fine. I've known a whole pack of dogs to come in here, but he never comes to any harm. He's my sister's son.'

I was relieved to hear her mentioned.

'Where is your sister?' I asked.

'She's dead.'

Ntombi put the brush aside and crouched by the fireplace. I sat down on the blankets next to the boy, wondering if I should comfort him. But there was no expression on his face, as he gazed out of the doorway as though looking after the dog's tracks. I looked back at Ntombi, watched her prepare a fire with dried reeds. The lack of consideration she showed for the child, the poverty and bleakness of the home, I felt myself judging her. But how could I judge her, a girl no older than I was? My own life seemed easy in comparison.

'Have you got any other family?' I asked, careful to keep my tone neutral.

'No,' she said, lifting a pot of water onto the fire.

'What about Wanda?' I asked.

She turned to face me and said, 'I told you, he's my sister's son.'

'Yes, but…,' I paused to consider my words. 'I just mean he seems quite young to be here on his own.'

She shrugged and said, 'The baker doesn't want him at the bakery, and I can't take him to school. Besides, Wanda's fine out here. I think he prefers dogs to people.'

I was shocked at how dismissive she was of her nephew's needs, shocked that anyone could think a toddler could look after themselves. She stood up and came to fetch the bowl, pausing to stroke Wanda's hair; the first sign of affection I'd seen her show him.

'This is our last bowl now, Wanda,' she said to him. 'After we've had tea, I'll make you more porridge.'

He glanced briefly at her as she spoke, before turning to look back out of the door.

She rinsed the bowl and filled it with lukewarm tea, handing it to me.

'Thank you,' I said, and took a sip.

The boy edged in closer, looking at the bowl. I held it to his mouth, tilting it so he could drink.

'I know it's not much,' Ntombi said, looking around her home, 'but I built it myself.'

I looked at her and smiled, seeing the pride on her face.

As we passed the tea between us, she talked in detail about each stage of building; how long she had worked at the bakery to get the materials she needed, and how she had forged enough for the furniture she had. Every so often I offered words of encouragement to hide my true feelings. Living out in the wilderness, in a shack barely visible from the river, a barren place where no one came, I wondered if I was the only person who knew they were out here. I considered they were poorer even than the beggars, who were at least offered donations of food. Aside from me, I wondered if Wanda had ever seen another face, except for Ntombi's; I wondered how growing up, isolated, with dogs for company had affected him. The look of detachment on his face stayed with me as I made my way back to town.

Chapter 8

My own troubles had faded into the background whilst in Ntombi's company, but now as I was heading home they resurfaced; my afternoon with Ntombi and Wanda was an added complication. I had never been gone so long before, and began to fret what Mata would say if she found out where I'd been. I mulled over possible explanations but all were fraught with lies. By the time I reached the river I had resolved only to consider my predicament at a later time.

Crossing the bridge, I saw Nisrin, waist deep in the water, perfectly still, with hand poised and clutching a knife. In one swift movement, her attacking hand plunged into the water, spearing an unsuspecting fish. I met her as she waded back to the bank, where she threaded the fish onto a hook with five others.

'We were wondering where you'd got to,' she said, reaching for my hand.

I smiled nervously.

'Come on, time for home,' she said. 'Mata's probably got a fire going by now.'

I was relieved she asked no awkward questions. Instead, as we walked home, she chatted about sea fishing, and how ridiculous she thought it was that the people of Shendi never tried it.

'Being afraid of the sea,' she said. 'It's crazy. I mean, how do people think anyone lives on the ocean if it's so dangerous?'

I nodded and commented in places, happy for her to keep talking, while I tried to think up an excuse for where I'd been all afternoon;

Mata was sure to ask. But nothing plausible seemed to stick and, in the end, I just had to hope that Nisrin would be enough of a distraction.

Turning into the street to home, I saw the mule harnessed to the cart still loaded with our wares. Mata always made sure the cart was unloaded as soon as we returned from market, but the door of the house was closed and there was no sign of her. I untied the mule from the harness, and led her to the trough, while Nisrin opened the door and went to look inside. She came back out a moment later.

'I'm sure she'll be back soon,' she said. 'We'd better get this cart unloaded.'

Her tone was casual but I saw her frown, before she turned away from me, busying herself with the cart.

'Where is she?' I asked.

'Maybe she forgot something,' Nisrin said, focused on untying the rope. 'She probably just lost track of time. I'm sure it's nothing to worry about.'

We unloaded the cart and lit a fire. Nisrin softly hummed as she seasoned the fish with spices and cooked them in a skillet. I sat on the doorstep looking out into the street, anxiously awaiting Mata's return.

'Come on in,' Nisrin said. 'Dinner's ready.'

I stood up and went to the table, where two plates were served.

'Shouldn't we wait for Mata?' I asked.

'I've kept some back for her,' Nisrin said with a smile. 'It's late, we should eat.'

The fish was tasty, but, worried about Mata, I had little appetite. My thoughts drifted to Ntombi and the child, thinking of them sharing a bowl of porridge. After a few mouthfuls, I pushed the food around my plate.

'Shall I tell you about the pearl I gave you?' Nisrin said, breaking the quiet.

I looked at her and nodded.

She put her fork down and said, 'It all started with my marriage proposal.'

'You're getting married!'

'Not if I can help it, but he's a persistent old man. Still, I suppose I'm not so young myself anymore.' She pushed the plate aside and rested her elbows on the table. 'The raft people consider any woman older than twenty to be 'past it', which suits me. I've never understood the point of marriage.'

'Why?' I asked.

'Well for one thing I prefer my independence,' she said. 'From what I've seen, that's the first thing to go when a woman gets married.'

'My mother never lost her independence,' I said. I paused, wondering what Nisrin knew about my father.

'You're mother's a remarkable woman,' she said. She reached across for my hand. 'Where was I?'

'Your marriage proposal.'

She nodded. 'So, of course I told him no: aside from having no interest in marriage, he's thirty years older than me and a drunk since his first wife died. But he wouldn't take no for an answer. So I set him what I thought was an impossible challenge, my hand in marriage for an oyster pearl; you only find them in the southern reefs, a shark-infested place. He must have got one of his sons to get it, because sure enough he presented it to me two days later.'

'What are you going to do now?'

She smiled and said, 'Well, I suppose I'll just have to come up with something truly impossible!'

I had thought the pearl was a beautiful stone; now it held less appeal. Two days ago the world had seemed simpler; but now I was starting to see the value of my ignorance. I looked over to the window to see it was now dark, and rubbed my eyes, pained by a headache.

'It's late,' Nisrin said. 'You should go to bed. I'll wait up for Mata.'

I stood up from the table and kissed her cheek.

'Thank you for supper,' I said.

I sank down onto the bed, curled up in the blanket, staring at the door, until drifting to sleep.

I stirred with the sound of the door softly closing, followed by Nisrin and Mata's hushed voices.

'Where have you been?' I said, rubbing sleep from my eyes.

Mata walked towards me, stiff as though in pain, holding onto her side as she slowly sat on the bed.

'You're hurt,' I said, sitting up.

'No, I'm fine.' She kissed me on the cheek. 'I'm just going down to the cellar with Nisrin for a while. Go back to sleep.'

'Why, what's happened?'

'Nothing. Go back to sleep.'

I stared into her eyes as she pulled the blanket over my shoulders, willing her to tell me that everything was okay, but her silence told me it wasn't. I watched her disappear with Nisrin behind the tapestry, listened to their footsteps on the cellar steps. Then, with the blanket pulled tight around my shoulders, I crept over to the tapestry and crouched on the floor, listening as they talked long into the night.

Mata said, 'I went to look for Sisile; she wasn't home and her house had been ransacked. The town guards came and found me there. Said they were arresting me for witchcraft. They pulled a hood over my head and dragged me out into the back of a cart. I couldn't see a thing but I know these streets. They took me into the alleys on the south side, into one of the storage buildings. Bastards tied me to a chair and whipped me.'

I clenched my teeth and gulped back the tears. I was afraid to hear more, afraid to know that my mother had been hurt; she could have been killed. But I had to know. I leaned closer to the tapestry, ear pressed against the coarse fabric as I strained to hear.

Mata said, 'They kept on with the same questions: what was I doing at Sisile's house; why did I go to the fields at night; how long have I been a witch? I denied everything and they just kept whipping me.'

'How did you get away?' Nisrin asked.

'They let me go. They couldn't prove anything.'

'Mata, you've got to leave,' Nisrin said. 'They could come here. What if they find your cellar? Come with me to the rafts. You and Suni can make a new life for yourselves.'

'I'm not leaving,' Mata said. 'This is my homeland; I won't let them drive me away.'

Chapter 9

I opened my eyes and turned onto my side, expecting to see Mata lying beside me, but I was alone in the bed. I'd barely slept; my sleep plagued with nightmares. I looked around the room now lit by the soft colours of dawn. The dishes were still left out on the table, and I was wearing the same clothes from the day before. Slowly I ordered my thoughts and felt my stomach churn with anxiety, remembering what I'd overheard.

Eyes on the tapestry I got out of bed and went to it, but as I reached out to pull it aside, my hand stopped short, hanging in the air. I felt like an intruder in my own home. It was quiet downstairs. I wanted to go down and wake them, talk to Mata, but I was afraid she'd be angry with me for listening in. *I* was angry, at her and for her. The life she led was too dangerous but she wouldn't listen, not to Nisrin, not to Faru; not to me. There was a barrier between me and my mother that I didn't know how to break.

I turned my back to the tapestry to look around the room. As my eyes rested on a pile of bowls on the shelf, my thoughts turned to Ntombi. I longed for company, for distraction from my worries. It was still early, barely morning; if I went now I could catch her before she left for work, and be back for when Mata woke. At least Ntombi would be pleased to see me, and she'd appreciate some bowls to replace those the dog had broken. I took one last look at the tapestry before I gathered my things and left.

The streets were quiet, the houses dark, but I kept my hood dipped low over my eyes and hurried onto the river. Over the bridge and out across wasteland, I approached Ntombi's shack and peered through the open door. There was no sign of her, only Wanda sitting huddled in a blanket.

'Hello, Wanda,' I said.

He stared at me, silent.

'You remember me, I'm your aunt's friend,' I said, as I stepped inside and put the bowls on the table.

I went to him and crouched down, holding my hands out to him. I wanted to comfort him, although he didn't appear to need comforting. I'd never met a child so detached from human contact before. Still, he gave no resistance when I sat down and lifted him onto my knee. When he leaned back against my chest, I rocked to and fro; before long, the rhythmic motion lulled him to sleep. I leaned back into the blankets, cradling him in my arms as I stared at the doorway waiting for Ntombi to return. As time wore on, I closed my eyes and felt myself drift.

I awoke, squinting from the bright sun shining through the door. Ntombi was crouched by the fire, stirring a pan.

'I must have fallen asleep,' I said, gently placing Wanda, still sleeping, down onto the blanket.

She turned her head and nodded, glancing briefly at me before turning back to the fire. I shifted nervously, embarrassed to be found having made myself at home without an invitation.

'Thanks for the bowls,' she said.

There was something odd about the tone of her voice. I wondered if she was annoyed at me for simply walking in when she wasn't home.

'I didn't mean to fall asleep,' I said. When she didn't answer, I stood up to leave. 'I shouldn't have come. I'm sorry.'

She lifted the pan off the fire and set it on the table.

'I'm glad you came,' she said, not meeting my eye as she stirred the porridge. 'This is ready. Stay and eat with us.'

'Thanks, but I should get home. My mother will wonder where I am.'

She put down the ladle and looked at me with pity, her brow furrowing.

'There's trouble in town, Suni. You should stay here.'

I stared at her for a moment before running out, thoughts of Mata thumping inside my head.

It was approaching midday, but the river was abandoned. I ran over the bridge, seeing plumes of smoke drifting over the rooftops. My heart was pounding painfully in my chest as I veered into deserted streets, the air carrying the smell of burning and the sound of distant voices. The closer I came to home, the louder the voices grew, until I could make out the chanting:

'In the name of Orag, end witchcraft! Kill the witches!'

I ran faster, fists clenched, skidding to a stop when I rounded the corner to my street. My home was on fire, barricaded from the outside, flames licking up through the grass roof. A crowd of people were gathered outside, holding fiery torches up high and chanting their murderous words. I grabbed for the wall feeling my knees go weak, and screamed:

'MATA!'

The mob turned to look, pure hate on their faces. The chanting died down, my screaming stopped, as we stared at one another in a moment of confusion. I knew their faces, but nothing was familiar as the world seemed to slow into one unmoving frame. I felt a strange, cold sensation in the pit of my stomach. *She can't be dead.* But I knew my eyes did not deceive me. The threads of my life were unravelling; the world had fallen into chaos.

'Get her!' yelled a voice from the crowd.

I turned and ran from the mob, the raging fire, the smell of death, through streets I had known my whole life. It felt like a dream, distorted and confused, a place I didn't belong. I had only one thought, *Faru.* He would help me; he would wake me from this nightmare.

The shutters of Faru's house were still closed but the door was ajar. I ran into the darkened room and tripped, stumbling to my knees. I looked in horror at Faru lying on the ground, staring at me with lifeless eyes. His throat was a gaping wound, a dark stain of his blood pooled on the floor. Crouched on hands and knees, my stomach lurched and I vomited, leaving me shivering with cold. I staggered to my feet, hearing the voices of the mob drawing closer, and peered out through the open door. I took one last look at Faru before I fled, heading for the river.

Hearing the killers searching the streets, my legs pounded the ground, as though they had a will of their own. Crossing the bridge, I looked back, but no one was following. Over the bridge and out across wasteland, Ntombi was waiting for me in the doorway of her hut.

'They're dead; they're all dead,' I said, collapsing in her arms.

I saw Mata engulfed in flames, reaching out to me with a charred, blackened hand. I ran towards her, but with every step she drifted further away. Seeing flames scorch her skin and mutilate her body, I thought the haunting screams came from her, until my voice turned hoarse and throat sore. As my screams turned into cracked cries, I saw Ntombi's face looking down on me; the feel of her fingers tenderly stroking my hair; the gentle sound of her soothing voice. I stared into her eyes, too afraid to avert my gaze, too afraid to remember. She lifted my head and brought a bowl to my lips. I took a sip of the sweet tea, and felt tears spill down my cheeks.

'She's dead,' I whispered. 'My mother's dead.'

I lay helplessly in her arms and cried for Mata, Nisrin, Faru and myself. I was sure my heart would break but it kept on beating, and finally I was too exhausted even to cry. The world had changed shape, had cast me out; I was a fugitive from the only place I'd ever called home, alone in the world, like Ntombi.

There were no words that could comfort, but I felt the strength in her arms as she cradled me, saw the understanding in her eyes as she witnessed my despair.

'What happened to your family?' I whispered, clinging to her hand.

She looked into space and said, 'My mother died in childbirth when she was having me. My father never forgave me for killing her. He would beat me, say I was ugly, say I should never have been born. Nothing was good enough for him, not me, not his job. He blamed everything but himself.' She swallowed, then continued. 'He earned a good living as a guard, but he starting drinking and lost his job. I think my sister was the only thing he half cared about. She was beautiful, and he put all his hopes on her marrying well. He didn't know about her affair with a fishing boy, and the child she was carrying until he was born. That was the first time father hit her.' Ntombi fell silent. After a moment, she went on. 'He threatened to kill her baby, said no one need find out. She went mad, hitting him, screaming at him. He beat her to the ground and didn't stop, even after she was dead. I grabbed the baby and ran away to live begging on the streets. Father died last year; I think the drink finally killed him. That's when I started building this house.'

'You survived,' I said.

'So can you.'

'They'll come looking for me. If they find me they'll kill me; they might kill you too just for helping me.'

I closed my eyes, feeling the world close in around me, until a thought surfaced from the hopelessness; I still had a kinsman left in the world.

'I have to go to my father,' I said.

Chapter 10

Dusk was falling as I sat in the doorway of Ntombi's shack. Keeping watch in the direction of town, seeing the rooftops as mere specks in the distance, I felt numb.

Ntombi draped a shawl over my shoulders and sat down beside me.

'Where is your father?' she asked.

I looked at her and said, 'He works at the mines.'

'The mines?' she said, eyes wide. 'You can't go there. Miners are loyal to the King. Your mother was accused of witchcraft... There of all places, it's not safe for you.'

'I have no choice,' I said quietly. 'I can't stay here, and I've got nowhere else to go. He's my father; he'll protect me. I have to believe that.'

'But it's not possible,' she said. 'Only guards and miners can enter the mountains, and only boys work the mines.'

I clenched my jaw, staring into her eyes. We had only just met, but my life was in her hands. And I trusted her, had heard her bare all. She went to school with children who were my enemy, but she was my friend, an outsider who kept her own council and did what she had to do to survive. I could only hope I might find her courage.

'Then I need a disguise,' I said. 'No one's looking for a boy.'

She looked at me, her eyes narrowed, before turning away to look out across the landscape.

'Please, Ntombi. I need your help. I don't even know how to get there.'

After a moment she looked back and said, 'Are you sure about this?'

'I'm not sure about anything,' I said. 'But it's the best I've got.'

She slowly nodded and said, 'Boys go by wagon to the mines. There's a pick-up in the morning, outside school.' She reached up to touch my long hair, her eyes travelling down the length of my smock as she stood up and offered me her hand. 'It's getting late. If we're going to do this, we should make a start.'

I took her hand and followed back inside.

We worked long into the night, cutting my hair short and transforming my smock into shorts. Ntombi's quietly assertive charge was reassuring, and her own personal story of courage, inspiring. I was surrounded by the enemy, but I had a father; for Ntombi, her own father had been the enemy. With each lock of hair that fell, and each stitch that was sewn, I told myself if she could survive, so could I.

As first light dawned, my transformation was complete.

'Well,' I said, 'how do I look?'

She put her hands on my shoulders and said, 'Like a boy.'

I leaned into her embrace, felt her arms around my back as I wrapped mine around her waist. I didn't want to let go; the thought of going on alone filled me with dread. It was Ntombi's courage that had kept me going throughout the night. I nestled my cheek against hers, slowly turned my head brushing my lips across her soft skin. She pulled away from me, wary and confused.

'I'm afraid,' I said.

'I know.'

'Will you come with me, to the wagon?' I asked.

She nodded.

They're not looking for a boy, I reminded myself, as we stepped outside leaving Wanda still sleeping.

Approaching the riverbank, seeing guards sleeping in the reeds among empty ale bottles, I felt a sickly feeling rise up from my stomach and swallowed back the urge to vomit. I clutched Ntombi's hand as we stole over the bridge, alert to every snore, every rustle of movement. By the time we reached the edge of town, I was retching, my body doused in a cold sweat. I leaned against the wall, grateful for

Ntombi's hand pressed against my clammy brow, as I hung my head to be sick.

Footsteps were heading our way, followed by a man's voice: 'What's going on here?'

I wiped my mouth and looked at the guard staring down at me with cold eyes.

'Filthy urchin; I should make you clean that up,' he said.

'Sorry,' Ntombi said, moving to stand in front of me. 'My brother's off to the mines today; he's just nervous at leaving home.'

'Can't your brother speak for himself,' he said, peering at me over Ntombi's shoulder.

I kept my head lowered, avoiding his eye, as Ntombi said, 'He's mute, but he's a good worker.'

'Deaf as well by the looks of it,' he said. 'That's all we need, another useless waif down there. Well, get on with you or you'll miss the wagon.'

Ntombi put her arm over my shoulder and bundled me away down the street. All through town the smell of burning lingered in the air. Nothing was familiar, only grotesque, and I longed to be far away.

A group of boys were gathered outside the school. Among them I saw faces I recognised; boys who had thrown stones and called me names. One boy was watching and giggling, nudging his friend to look. I tightened my grip on Ntombi's hand but she prized herself free and stepped back. The boys lost interest and turned to join another group.

'Just relax,' Ntombi whispered. 'No one recognises you.'

When two camel-driven wagons arrived, drivers alighted and divided the boys into two groups. Ntombi ushered me forwards to join a group, where I was swept up in a wave of bodies, all clambering up into the wagon. I turned for a final look, saw Ntombi put a finger to her chin and tilt her head up, a gesture that told me to be strong. As I was pushed forward into the wagon, losing sight of her, I only hoped I could find the courage to survive what lay ahead. I clambered to an empty seat at the front and sat down on the hard wooden bench. As the whips cracked and the wagons set off with a jolt, I tried to imagine my father's face.

Crammed into the wagons like goats, it was hot as an oven. I leaned my head against the side of the wagon, feeling every jolt as we rumbled through the streets of town. The boys chatted excitedly, paying me no attention as they shared aspirations of the fortune soon to be theirs. But by the time we reached the edge of the fields, the reality of our situation was sinking in. Thin slits between the wooden slats provided only teasing wisps of fresh air. Seeing civilization slip away as we entered the desert, breathing in the stuffy air thick with the smell of musty sweat, the boys fell silent.

Sweat was pouring from my brow, but my insides felt cold and hollow. I pressed my face against the wagon, helpless to stop silent tears from falling. I had never been so far from home. *I have no home.* I closed my eyes and pictured Mata's face. *I thought you'd never leave me but you did.*

I felt betrayed; she had chosen her beliefs over me. And now I was betraying her. Unless… I thought about all she had said about my father, how he had claimed there was another way. What if he was right? Maybe he *had* found a way to spread the word of the Mantra amongst non-believers. Mata had done no better; getting killed, abandoning me, had achieved nothing. It felt like taking sides, siding with the man she couldn't bring herself to even talk about for years. But if he was right, maybe her quest didn't have to die with her. I looked out between the slats, watched the meandering contours of the desert rise and fall with towering sand-dunes. Listening to the low, grumbling breaths of the camels walking alongside, I mercifully drifted off.

I woke as the wagon slowed to a stop. As the boys clambered out, I followed and saw we were still in the middle of the desert. My stomach was aching with the need to urinate. Seeing boys scatter to relieve themselves, I envied them their freedom. I sat down, dangling my legs over the edge of the wagon, trying to act casual when two drivers came heaving a barrel of water between them. With only one mug, they drank in turn, then filled it again, offering it to me. I was surprised by the gesture and concluded that driving must be a lowly job. My mouth felt as dry as sand, but I dared only sip the warm water enough to take the edge off my thirst.

The boys were returning to the wagon. I passed the cup on, careful not to meet anyone's eye. As they shared the water between them, no one paid me much attention, until I realised one boy was walking straight towards me; he was the boy who had called me a witch at the river.

'No one's seen you before,' he said, his tone unfriendly. 'What's your name?'

Name? I hadn't thought of a name. My mind went blank and I stared down at the ground.

He shoved my shoulder and said, 'Don't ignore me!'

Other boys were moving in behind him.

'You simple or something?' he said. 'Don't even know your own name?'

He shoved me again and then grabbed hold of my wrist, holding up my arm and laughing.

'Look at the state of him,' he said to the other boys. 'There's not enough muscles on these skinny arms to shift pebbles.' He slapped me on the head and said, 'Look at me!'

I pulled my arm from his grip and raised my head to meet his eye.

'My father's at the mines,' I said. 'So you'd better not touch me again.'

His eyes narrowed, uncertain. For a moment I thought I'd said enough.

'He probably works in the kitchen,' he said, his cold stare fixed on me.

The rest of the boys all laughed out loud, until the driver pushed his way through and cuffed the boy on the back of the head.

'That's enough,' the driver said. 'Get back to your seats. I'll not have trouble on my wagon.'

The boy pushed me aside as the rest climbed in, forcing me to board last. I climbed up and clambered through to my seat, aware that everyone was watching. I tripped and fell in the aisle, saw the boy's leg deliberately stuck out. I got up and finally found my seat, feeling sick with the thought I had made an enemy.

The line of the horizon transformed into great mountainous peaks, cloaked in shades of orange with the setting of the sun. It was almost dark by the time we reached the first slopes on a path that abruptly grew steep. In the shadow of splintering crags and sheer cliff faces we meandered narrow paths, the soft thumps of the camels' padded feet, and occasional whip cracks echoing around deep canyons. Like the desert, this was a barren landscape. I thought of the stories I had grown up with, thought of the picture my great grandmother had painted, and imagined a time when people had climbed these same mountain passes on a pilgrimage, imagined their footsteps still echoing where camels now trod.

Two beacons shone bright, guiding the wagons to the gateway to the mines. Entering the gate between two tall towers, we arrived in a high-walled courtyard. We climbed out of the wagons, stiff and weary, and were jostled by the drivers to stand in line. A wooden door set in the mountains opened, and a man came out. He was a foreboding figure, tall and stocky, with well-groomed clothes, combed hair and beard, and stern, deep-set eyes. He said little as he moved down our line, inspecting height, arm girth, hands and teeth; what few words he did utter were spoken with quiet authority that no one dared disobey. I was standing at the end of the line, my eyes watering from the effort of not wetting myself. Thinking what would happen if my disguise was uncovered, I reached up to find reassurance in my cropped hair.

'Stand still!' the man said, grabbing my chin.

As he pulled my mouth open to check my teeth, I saw his face up close and noted that his features didn't resemble my own.

'My name is Gusta,' he said, once he had finished with me. 'You will all call me sir. You're miners now, in my charge. Follow me.'

He led the way through the door into the mountains, down a labyrinth of dark tunnels intermittently lit by torchlight. The air was stuffy and the rancid smell, like nothing I'd known before: the stale odour of decay, sweat and human excrement. I put a hand over my mouth and nose as we were taken deep into the belly of the mines, where we arrived at a chamber strewn with threadbare mattresses.

'This is your home now,' Gusta said. 'Get some sleep. Work starts early in the morning.'

Watching him leave it dawned on me, just as no one could enter the mines uninvited, no one was free to leave. The mountains held a power that could swallow children whole.

Chapter 11

The mood in the chamber was bleak, as everyone stood silently staring at their feet. Only one spirit managed to rise from the quagmire, the boy I had made an enemy of on the wagon.

'This'll do,' he said, dropping his knapsack down onto a mattress next to the wall. He turned to look back at the rest of us. 'What's wrong with you all? We're miners now; we'll be rich!'

'Sbo's right,' another boy said. 'The Earth Spirit Orag provided the crystals, and we'll be the men who dig them.'

Taking strength from this self-appointed leadership, agreement slowly rippled throughout the group. While romantic notions of heroism were revived, I edged away towards a mattress in the far corner of the cave. A warm, damp sensation was trickling down my legs and I was mortified to realise that, despite my best efforts, I was wetting myself. The independence in my movements didn't go unnoticed.

'You think you're too good for the rest of us,' Sbo said, striding across the chamber towards me. He dropped his gaze, eyes opening wide when he saw the growing pool at my feet. 'He's pissed himself!' He turned to look back at the boys. 'Look at this.'

Laughter sounded throughout the chamber. Sbo came closer, his mouth turned up into a cruel smirk as he prodded me in the shoulder.

'What, you missing your mother or something?' he said.

His words lit a fire in my belly. *I have no mother; thanks to people like you.* All the grief and despair exploded into anger, as I clenched my hand into a fist and punched Sbo in the face, so hard it knocked him to the ground. The world became a blur. I jumped on top of Sbo, hitting him again and again, to the sound of my mother's screams ringing inside my head.

I felt a hand grab the scruff of my neck and lift me off Sbo. Hanging upright, mid-air, my feet barely brushed the ground as I looked down at Sbo, seeing blood pouring from his nose.

It was Gusta's quietly chilling voice that spoke: 'Anyone got anything to say?'

Among the astonished faces of the boys, no one spoke.

'Get yourself cleaned up,' Gusta said to Sbo, before turning around, still holding me out in front. 'Any more trouble in here and I'll have you all in pits.'

I was frogmarched out of the chamber and along the winding passageway. Without warning Gusta swung me to the side. I closed my eyes, expecting to be slammed into the wall; instead, the ground disappeared beneath my feet and I was dropped into a deep pit.

'We'll see if you still want to cause trouble after a night in the pit,' Gusta said.

I watched helplessly as he dragged a board over to cover the hole, heard a heavy thud, like a rock being rolled. Then there was silence in the pitch black.

I stood up and reached, feeling the wooden board. I pushed against it, but it was solid. I tried again, balancing on tiptoes to gain height, but it didn't move.

'Let me out!' I shouted, feeling panic rising.

I banged against it with my fists. No one came but I kept banging, until I felt a thick splinter drive deep into my hand.

I pulled the splinter out with my teeth, tasting blood. Aside from the sound of my breathing, there was silence. I sank to my knees, staring into the dark with wide eyes. I had feared the guards all my life, had known all those who worked for the King to be my enemy, and now, of my own volition, I had walked straight into the heart of that enemy. *What have I done?* I buried my face in my hands but I was too exhausted to cry. Somewhere in the dark recesses lingered Mata's prayer, but for now, enemy or not, my father was my only hope.

It felt a long time coming and by the time Gusta returned, I was a lonely shadow with hollow eyes absorbing the darkness.

'Have you learnt your lesson?' he said, holding the board poised to slam back down.

'Yes,' I said, my voice weak.

He reached down for my hand and hauled me out. After the dark cramped hole my body was stiff and my eyes hurt in the torchlight, but I was barely given a chance to get to my feet before he led me on through an endless maze of tunnels. This underground world rang with the sound of picks hammering against rock as we passed groups of boys hard at work, watched over by men sitting idly by. I looked at the faces of boys who crossed our path, struggling to push carts filled with debris. Seeing their faces lifeless and ashen, I wondered when they had last seen the light of day; would they ever see it again? Deep beneath the earth, the sun was a distant memory; already my eyes were used to the dark.

Gusta stopped at a worksite. One by one, boys I recognised from my sleeping chamber paused hammering as they turned to look. My gaze lingered on Sbo, shocked to see his swollen black eye.

'I've got another one for you, son,' Gusta said to an older boy watching over the group. He pushed me forward. 'Watch out for him though: he started a fight last night. Anymore trouble, just put him back in the pit.'

'Well?' the boy said to me, once Gusta had left. He stepped closer, leaving me facing his bare chest. 'Are you planning to cause trouble?'

I shook my head.

He pushed my head back, forcing me to look up into his narrowed eyes that looked out from beneath the lip of a cap pulled low over his face.

'My name is Mandla,' he said. 'And you take orders from me now.'

He stepped aside, leaving me facing Sbo backed up by several other boys.

Mandla looked from me to Sbo and said with a smirk, 'If you two have got unfinished business, sort it out now.'

'Go on Sbo,' the boys said, slapping him on the shoulder.

Sbo's stare was fixed on me, but he made no move.

'Go on, Sbo,' one boy said. 'What are you waiting for?'

I clenched my teeth, eyes locked on Sbo's as he took a step towards me and leaned in, his face close to mine.

'You caught me off guard last night,' he said. 'It was just a lucky punch. You won't be so lucky again.'

The tone of his voice was confident, but I saw the uncertainty in his eye as he looked away briefly when he spoke. A moment passed and he made no move.

Keeping my shoulders straight, eyes on Sbo's, I said, 'I'm not looking for a fight.'

His face softened for a moment; I imagined it was relief. *I* knew I wouldn't be so lucky to win again, but I suspected Sbo didn't. He shrugged his shoulders and took a step back.

A voice from the crowd said, 'Are you going to let him get away with it?'

'I'm not gonna waste my time with that,' Sbo said. He turned away and picked up his pick. 'Only nutters piss themselves.'

The boys watched as Sbo struck the rock, a moment of confusion before they started sniggering. Seeing them turn their backs, I quietly sighed with relief. I had earned the dubious respect of our ringleader and from that day forth, I was left alone.

A nearby trough filled with murky water was the only refreshment. Under Mandla's watchful eye I drank as long as I dared, and then grabbed a pick, finding a spot away from Sbo. I gripped the pick and swung, my arm reverberating as it hit rock. Blow after blow and only chips of stone fell away. Tired moans soon sounded throughout out group, but with Mandla pacing, a whip in his hand, our tired arms kept swinging. A single lash across one young boy's back was enough for everyone to get the message. Aside from sporadic whistling carried from further down the tunnel, there was silence among our group as exhaustion and misery set in.

As time dragged, my pile of rubble steadily grew. I worked hard. More than wanting to avoid the whip, I secretly aimed to please.

Finally, when my pile was bigger than anyone else's, I plucked up the courage to ask about my father.

I turned to face Mandla as he passed behind me, cowering when he raised the whip.

'I just want to ask if you know any men called Fazi here,' I said.

He brought the whip down into my side, a pain so sharp I fell to my knees.

'You don't get to speak,' he said, kicking me in the stomach. 'Now, get back to work.'

I struggled to my feet, leaning heavily on the pick. Staring at the rock I swallowed back the tears, clenching my jaw as I raised the pick and struck the rock again and again, until the ache in my arms was the only pain I could feel.

The day ended with a long march to the dining chamber. We filed in, passing an old man serving bowls of porridge from a huge vat. Group leaders sat at the head of long tables, and led the prayer:

'Earth Spirit Orag, we thank you for the gift of prosperity you bestow upon us. Humble before you, we vow to serve your messenger with obedience and devotion. We pledge our allegiance, and the allegiance of our sons and daughters. Now and forever, we are your followers.'

The chamber fell quiet, aside from the sound of spoons scraping the dishes clean. I swallowed back the bland meal, discretely checking the handful of grown men that came and went. I searched for facial features similar to my own, desperate to be rescued from this dark world, but among the crooked noses, squinting eyes and broad foreheads, I saw nothing familiar.

That night, I lay back on the thin mattress, listening to the boys' sombre chat as I stared into the fire of the torch on the far wall. The mines were vast, but my father, my only hope, was here, somewhere. After a hard day's labour, bravado was wearing thin, and quiet soon descended. When the sound of snoring rippled throughout the chamber, I sat up to lean on my elbow and looked around. No one stirred. I stood up and crept along the edge of the wall towards the entrance, peering out into the passageway. If I could just find the men, maybe I could find my father. I looked back into the chamber, remembering the pit, still feeling the sting of the whip. *You didn't survive the mob to spend the rest of your days pounding rock.* I set off down the quiet tunnel, right, left, left again, committing every turn to memory just as diligently as I had revised Mata's potions. *Mata;* I steeled myself, focused. Chambers came and went but all were filled with sleeping boys. Up ahead I thought I heard movement. I stopped, furtive. Stumbling footsteps were heading towards me. I crept back to a worksite and crouched behind a pile of stone. When an old man staggered on by I peered out, considering his crooked back and hunched shoulders. *He's too old to be my father.*

'What the…' I turned and saw a man looking straight at me. He lunged, grabbing my shoulder, and hauled me over the stone. 'What are you doing creeping about like a thief?'

'I'm not a thief,' I said, smelling ale on his breath as I got a close up view of his pointed chin. 'I'm looking for my father.'

'I haven't got time for this,' he said, dragging me along the passage where I was dropped into a pit more cramped than the first.

When light finally shone down into the pit, it was Gusta's face looking down at me.

'I might've known it was you,' he said, dragging me out. He hit me hard across the face, digging his fingers into my shoulder as he led me down the passage.

Back in the chamber, we found the boys stripped bare, dashing to and from an archway on the far side. Seeing bodies dripping wet, hearing the sound of splashing water, I was desperate to wash, but returned to my mattress and sat down. Once the boys were dressed, Gusta ordered us to stand in line. I kept my head lowered and positioned myself at the end of the row.

'What's wrong with you?' Gusta yelled, marching straight towards me. 'Get washed!'

He hit me and I stumbled. When he raised his hand again, I ducked and ran for the archway, smiling at the sight of troughs filled with water from underground springs. Out of sight of the entrance, I scrubbed myself clean, and relieved myself in a deep pit stinking in the corner. When I re-joined the line, half the boys' heads had already been shaved, apparently to prevent against head-lice. Once we were as bald as the day we had been born, there was no doubt; we were miners who belonged to the mountain and to the men who ran it.

Chapter 12

I suffered many beatings and spent more nights in the pit than I could count, but still I found no trace of my father. I had come in search of familiarity, but deep in the heart of its lair I saw only the face of my enemy. Though I had no name, my reputation for disobedience was soon widespread. I felt hope slipping away but still I hung on. Despite being closely watched day and night, I seized any opportunity to slip away. Finally Gusta decided on another tactic, announcing I was to work in the crystal caves.

It was a frightening thought, one I mulled over as Gusta led me on an unfamiliar route, branching from the main tunnels. Cave collapses were common; some boys had never returned, buried alive in the dark. The passageway narrowed, forcing Gusta to stoop as it spiralled down. I clambered down the steep uneven ground behind him, relieved when the walls opened out into a small chamber. A wizened old man was sitting on a chair in the corner, hunched over, peering into a rusty tin. When he saw us he snapped the tin shut, and looked up at me with squinted eyes.

'I've got you a replacement, Melrod,' Gusta said.

'I told 'em I needed someone small,' Melrod said. 'He's too big. He'll never fit through, not with the last lad still buried down there. He'll likely bring the whole lot down.'

He glanced at the wall that was pitted with holes, like over-sized wormholes; from somewhere inside the wall came the sound of scuffling. I looked at one hole with dust still spewing out, and thought about my predecessor, likely dead, buried in rubble. A light appeared in another hole, followed by the face of a young boy; he looked about eight or nine years old. He crawled on all fours to Melrod, stiff as though his body had set in that crouched position, and emptied handfuls of crystals from his pockets, pouring them into Melrod's tin. Seeing Gusta and Melrod focused on the boy, I took a step back: the thought of that wall becoming my tomb was unbearable.

'Where do you think you're going?' Gusta said, reaching back and grabbing my shoulder.

I watched the boy disappear back into the hole, sick with the thought that I was soon to follow.

'This one's been nothing but trouble,' Gusta said to Melrod. 'At least down here we'll know where he is. And if he doesn't make it out, good riddance.' He pushed me forward. 'Any more of your tricks down here, and I'll have you whipped like a dog.'

Melrod handed me a lantern and pointed a stick at the dust-filled hole.

'Well, get on with it,' he said. 'Follow that down to the cave, and don't come back without crystals. There's plenty down there.'

Reluctantly, I took the lantern, peered into the pitch black cavity and, with gritted teeth, climbed in.

My breaths were soon laboured from the dust and growing panic, my hands and knees grazed, as I squeezed through the tight tunnel with no notion of how far I had to go. Every so often I stopped to catch my breath and to listen, fearing further rock-fall, wondering if I might hear a cry in the dark from a boy still alive. I kept focused on the lantern light, my only ally, and saw I was approaching a pile of rubble blocking the way ahead. Holding the lantern steady in one hand, with the other I carefully shifted stones to clear the way.

My fingers touched something smooth and soft. I pulled my hand back and slowly brought the lantern closer. I saw the dead boy's face, his eyes closed, and his open mouth filled with dirt. Fearing it was a reflection of my own fate, I quickly put a stone back over the face, not wanting to see. I clenched my jaw, refusing to cry. Tears were of no use; the only way out was with crystals. I lifted the lantern to inspect the gap I had made; it was narrow but passable. Holding the lantern by

59

the handle gripped between my teeth, I climbed up the rubble and over the other side.

Feeling stone shift beneath me, I reached out with my hands but there was nothing sturdy to hold onto. I slid down the rubble, head first, holding my hands out to break my fall. My knees hit solid ground but my hands touched only air as I hurled forward, looking down over a steep rock face. Knees anchored, the lantern swinging from my teeth, I clung to stone outcrops and slowly inched back from the sheer drop. I sank back on my ankles, put the lantern down, and stared out into the dark. As my panicked breaths gradually slowed I was left with cold clarity; I was beyond fear, beyond despair; finally I thought I had reached the end.

'I'm going to die down here,' I whispered.

A cold sensation washed over me, strangely familiar. I thought back to the day of the fire, the feeling of cold detachment I'd felt knowing I would never see my mother again. I closed my eyes to stop the tears from falling, wishing I could see her face, feel her skin, hug her one last time.

'You were right,' I whispered, imagining Mata could hear me. 'There's nothing for me here. You were always right.'

'You're *my* daughter.'

I opened my eyes. It couldn't be. *Mata?*

'Suni.'

I reached for the lantern and held it up. My mother was there, an apparition floating mid-air beyond the ledge, just out of reach. Her mouth was moving as though she was speaking, but now there was silence. She held out her hand as though beckoning me to her, smiling as she slowly sank from sight. I crawled forward, holding out the lantern, and realised I had emerged mid-way up the walls of a huge ovoid cave, the walls disappearing up into the dark, the lantern light showing the tips of stalactites hanging down. The walls curved to meet the ground below, where Mata was looking up from among rocky stalagmites. Gripping the lantern in my teeth, I inched my way over the edge and climbed down.

Up close I saw crystals embedded in the walls, shimmering in the lantern light. When my feet touched solid ground, I turned and saw my mother drifting deeper into the cave. I followed, weaving around rocks, struggling to keep up with her. She stopped some way ahead, her back to me as she held out an arm, hand pressed against the wall. Seeing her image slowly fading I ran to reach her, but by the time I arrived she was gone.

'Mata?' I said, willing her to come back to me, moving the lantern from side to side, searching for a sign.

I couldn't see her, but with the familiar cold washing through me, I felt her guiding me. I held the lantern close to the wall, looking at where she had placed her hand; one crystal was bigger and shining brighter than the rest. I brushed a hand over it, felt the surrounding stone crumble beneath my fingers. I dug down, prising it free, and held it up to the light. Colours shone out from the milky white stone, mesmerizing tones of red, blue, yellow and green. I inspected it from every angle, held it in the palm of my hand; it was a stone so big, I could barely close my fingers around it. The cold feeling of Mata's presence had left me, but holding a stone she had guided me to, I felt safe in the knowledge I would never be alone again. I clutched it close to my chest. The crystal was a gift from my mother and I would not be parted from it.

I considered hiding the crystal in the cave, but quickly decided against it. I had no way of knowing whether I would be sent back here, or whether this cave linked to any other tunnel. Somehow I had to get it past Melrod. I fingered the folds and clumsy stitches of my smock, and found a loose hem. I slid the crystal inside, and then set to work gathering more, hoping that if I took Melrod enough, he wouldn't be suspicious.

I emerged from the tunnel to find Melrod and Gusta with a group of young boys.

'You took your time,' Melrod said, holding out the tin. 'We'd just about given up on you.'

I emptied my pockets into the tin, and sat still while he prodded and poked, checking my pockets, hands, mouth and ears. But he didn't find my crystal.

Late that night, when the boys were sleeping, I lay curled on my mattress rolling the crystal in my fingers. I longed to see the rainbow of colours that had appeared in the lantern light, but with only a dim light from across the room the stone was lost in darkness. I closed both hands around it and held it against my chest, remembering Mata's face.

My hands were growing strangely warm, as though heat was coming from within the gem. I held it out to look and was surprised to see a white light, flickering like a candle in the centre of the crystal. I pulled the blanket over my head, afraid that someone might see. Looking into the light, I thought back to the dream Mata had told me about; here I was, in a dark place, looking into a strange light. My mother had been a seer. She had seen my future. I gazed into the crystal, wondering what it all meant.

The light grew stronger, radiating out from the crystal. Patterns formed in the white glow, as shades of blue appeared, swirling like ink in water, mixing to form a nimbus of silvery grey. The colour grew stronger, appearing opaque, like mist, and felt cool to the touch; it was a familiar cold, like I had felt in Mata's presence. The cool mist enveloped my hands, crept over my wrists and up my arms. As it moved across my chest, washing over my face, the feel of the mattress fell away. I felt like I was floating, in a place I couldn't see beyond the thick mist, and wondered whether I had strayed into a dream.

I gained a sense of orientation when I felt solid ground beneath my feet and realised I was standing upright. In this silent place, cool mist was swirling all around, revealing tones in the grey. The first face I saw frightened me; it was the face of a man, walking past as though he didn't see me. The second face was closer, a woman I realised was a ghost. She too came and went as though oblivious to my presence. I watched and waited, seeing more ghosts drift by, willing my mother to reveal herself. She did, just beyond my reach, a fleeting appearance that came and went in the mist.

The mist was clearing, the air was growing warmer. My legs were still but I felt myself drift, until I opened my eyes and found myself lying on the mattress, the crystal still clutched in my fingers. I stared into it, willing the light to return, wanting to see my mother again. But the light would not come. All the next day I thought about my crystal, wondering whether the strange world of mist would reveal itself to me again, wondering if I would see Mata again. It did, that night, and each night thereafter.

I had never believed I had a gift, never believed I held the key to the Mantra's return. I still didn't. It was Mata; it had always been her. She had a gift, even after death. Part of me wanted to believe she had found her way back to offer comfort, but I knew my mother: her unwavering faith in the Mantra, her lifelong devotion to see its return. She had come back to me to show me how. I had been lost, but not now; now I would follow the path my mother laid for me. I was determined to understand, determined to see what she wanted to reveal, determined to see her dreams realised.

Days turned into months and months into a year or more. My developing body was the only indication of passing time and this I managed to successfully conceal, stealing any pieces of cloth I could find to strap down my growing chest and absorb my sporadic menstrual cycle. In the mornings I became well-practised at rising before the gongs sounded, and in this way I could wash and dress without suspicion from my peers.

In every aspect of life in the mines, I kept to myself; in return the boys paid me little notice. Still I couldn't help but see the effect that a humdrum existence of hard labour and uncompromising routine had on the boys' spirits. Infected by the darkness, the colour in their faces turned to ash and the spark in their eyes threatened never to return.

My own eyes grew ever more naive to the light of the outside world. I had given up hope of finding my father and lost any ambition to keep trying. The mines were lost in darkness, where no true word of the Mantra had been spread, the miners, followers only of Orag. But I had my crystal, safely buried in my mattress. It was this light that I looked to, and the world of mist it revealed. My mother was always waiting for me there, guiding me further each time. Her life's quest was now my own and patiently I explored the mist, waiting for answers to be revealed.

Chapter 13

Hard calluses formed on my hands and knees from crawling through the narrow tunnels, and many times over I narrowly escaped being trapped under rock fall. But still I worked hard to maintain a plentiful supply of crystals: working in the caves meant I had little contact with others. Still no one knew I was a girl, and seclusion felt to be the surest way of keeping it secret.

However, late one evening Gusta made an unexpected visit to our chamber, bringing with him an end to my solitude. Following closely at his heels was a young boy; he appeared no more than five years old, much younger than any boy I had seen in the mines before. I wondered where he could have come from. I hadn't heard of any wagons arriving and besides, if there had been a fresh intake there would be others; this child appeared alone in every sense. Shrinking back in Gusta's shadow he held a furtive expression, wild in nature like a prey animal wary of circling predators. With an untamed streak that neither expected approval nor felt self-pity, he appeared disconnected from the rest of the world; if nothing else, this I recognised.

Even Gusta showed a softer side that night. Instead of just leaving the child to fend for himself, he led him over to where the boys were gathered.

'I need someone to show him the ropes,' Gusta said.

No one answered, as every boy looked in any direction but at the new arrival. I was watching from the far corner. After a pause, Gusta looked across at me and brought the boy over.

'You,' Gusta said to me. 'Keep an eye on him.'

He turned and left the boy in my charge.

I had gone to great lengths to secure my solitude and guard my secret. A companion would surely be compromising, but Gusta was not someone to refuse, and besides, I couldn't help but pity the child.

'What's your name?' I asked.

He didn't answer, didn't even meet my eye.

I wondered if he might be deaf, but when I asked him to sit down, he did. I tilted his chin to see his face. When our eyes met, I was surprised to see his gaze linger, as though recognising something.

'You can sleep on here tonight,' I said. 'We'll find you a mattress in the morning.'

I hadn't expected him to be so trusting, but he lay down on my mattress, pulled his knees up to his chest, and closed his eyes. For a while I watched him sleep, saw the tension in his tightly clenched jaw, and instinctively felt the need to protect him.

The next morning, I awoke early as usual and went to wash while the boys were still sleeping. Standing in the cool stream of water, I turned to let it run down my back. The child was there, standing in the entrance, watching me. I grabbed for a towel to cover myself, but knew he had seen. I ran to him, crouching down to face him on his level.

'You mustn't tell anyone,' I whispered. 'No one can know I'm a girl. Do you understand?'

He simply nodded, as though nothing was amiss. I considered his gaze but it didn't falter. Since my young friend was yet to speak, I relaxed, trusting he would keep my confidence.

The child was too small to dig, so Gusta agreed he could work with me in the crystal caves. He had courage and never left my side, following through the dark tunnels. Even when the walls shook with the distant sound of rumbling, he looked to me. I had trained my hearing to detect warning signs, and while others fell victim to tunnel collapses, I kept us free from harm. But tunnel collapses were on the increase, and not just the in the warren surrounding the crystal caves. News of one of the main tunnels caving in brought a crushing blow to morale among the boys. But the names of the dead were spoken only in whispers. Discipline tightened and work continued.

The boy worked hard; the small, wiry proportions of his body delved easily into the earth, and over time his findings proved great. Still he didn't speak, not even to me, and I wondered if he could. Until, one night, I was witness to a curious encounter. He was lying on his mattress, watching a mouse peering out of a nearby hole. Mice were a common sight in the mines, though they never came close to people. But when the boy held out a beckoning hand, the mouse came scampering straight to him. It stopped, twitching its nose as though sniffing his fingers.

'Haraham, harahee, lulifey,' the boy whispered, strange sounds that to me held no meaning.

The mouse sat back on its hind legs, head cocked as though listening intently. This curious exchange continued for a while, until the boy gently stroked the mouse's head before it scampered away.

It was as Mata had told; remnants of the gifts remained. My young friend didn't speak to people but, each night, he spoke to mice in words of the old tongue. It was soon noticed that wherever the boy went, mice were always close by. I heard whispers among the other boys, calling the mice vermin and claiming the boy was cursed. Whenever they saw me listening, they quickly fell quiet: no one had forgotten my attack on Sbo, and since the boy was with me, he was left alone.

My bond with the boy grew; it was a bond that needed no words. I understood his expressions and gestures implicitly, with the familiarity of kin. Until one morning, when Gusta came for him. Gusta wouldn't tell me where he was taking the boy but, while I was anxious, the boy appeared impassive as he was led away. He was gone all that day and the next, brought back the following evening. Just as I had come to expect he said nothing, but like in the first days of knowing him, he returned with a sad, wary look in his eyes.

'Welcome back,' I said, placing a hand on his arm.

He flinched from my touch, holding his arm protectively against his chest.

I couldn't sleep that night, worrying about my friend. The next morning I insisted he show me his arm, and saw his elbow bruised and swollen.

'What happened?' I asked. 'Did you fall?' He shook his head. 'Did someone hurt you?'

He made no response, just appeared confused as he looked at me, a glazed expression in his eyes.

I wanted to keep him close, but Gusta kept coming back for him. Each time he was gone for two or three days, returning with more bruises. I pleaded with Gusta not to take him, or at least tell me where he was going, but he wouldn't tell me, just hit me for speaking out of line. Oddly the boy never tried to resist, and so it remained a disturbing mystery. I was forced to stand by as his sleep grew restless and he lost his appetite. It was only at night, when speaking to the mice, that he appeared at ease.

I never disturbed the private encounters between the mice and the boy, and in return I was offered the same respect; the crystal hidden in my mattress had not gone undetected from the boy's ever watchful eyes. It was an understanding that we both could trust, and for my part I remained free to search the mist, guided by my mother. The sight of her was a comfort, but wandering through the quiet mist felt aimless, with answers yet to be revealed. There were no markers in this undefined world, and I could never be sure how far I'd explored, or how long I had been gone. Though judging by how tired I was during the day, I was staying away for longer.

One morning, I returned to the feel of the physical world and looked around, checking the boys were still sleeping. All was quiet. I hid the crystal in my mattress and sank back, wanting to sleep. I closed my eyes but felt restless, worrying I had stayed away too long. A morning wash was refreshing, and something I didn't want to forfeit. I got up and crept over to the washroom, quickly undressed and stood beneath a stream of cool water. Head down, I scrubbed the dirt from my scalp.

'You're a girl!'

I grabbed the towel and wrapped it around me, stepping back from the stream. I didn't dare turn around, just stared at the wall trying to calm my panic. *He's only seen you from the side.* Cloaked over my shoulders, the towel covered down to my thighs.

'Hey Sbo!' I recognized Thani's voice. 'Come and look at this, I saw her, she's a girl.'

What do I do? I didn't dare move; my heart was racing as I heard more people come in.

'What you on about?' I heard Sbo say.

'That!' Thani said. 'She's a girl!'

'Oi you,' Sbo said. 'Turn round.'

'Don't be stupid,' I said, trying to sound confident as I clutched the towel.

'See,' Thani said. 'She won't.'

I willed them to leave, but footsteps came closer. I turned my head to see Sbo grab my arm.

'Get lost,' I said, trying to shake him off.

Thani joined him, yanking the towel free and shoving me round to face the crowd. Seeing their looks of astonishment, humiliation turned to dread. *They'll kill me if they find out who I am.*

As shock abated the boys closed in, shouting over one another: 'What's a girl doing here?' 'You been spying on us?' 'Freak!'

Sbo came to stand in front of me, his glare quietly chilling: for all this time he had remained beaten by a girl. Seeing him raise his hand I flinched, but he paused and dropped it back down by his side.

'You'd better tell us why you're here,' he said.

Naked, exposed as a girl, I felt utterly disarmed. But I straightened my shoulders and forced myself to look him in the eye.

'I told you, I came looking for my father,' I said.

'What's going on?' Gusta said, pushing his way through the crowd.

I tried in vain to cover myself with my hands, as he looked at me in astonishment. My mouth was too dry to speak; I was too afraid even to cry.

'She said she came looking for her father,' Sbo said. 'She's a liar.'

'So it seems,' Gusta said. I had expected anger, but his voice was surprisingly quiet. He was looking at me differently, his lips turned up into a faint smile. I had never seen him smile at all before. 'Well this is a turn up,' he said. 'You've been living in the wrong quarter. Get dressed, you're coming with me.'

The boys looked as confused as I felt. I quickly dressed, relieved to regain what little dignity I had left.

'I need my shoes,' I said, scurrying through and back to my mattress.

My young friend was waiting for me there, a meaningful look in his eyes that left me wondering what he knew that I didn't. I pulled my shoes on slowly, staring at the corner of the mattress. I didn't know where I was going, but I couldn't leave my crystal behind.

'Get a move on,' Gusta said, coming to stand over me.

The boy suddenly threw himself at me, wrapping his arms around my waist. I hugged him back.

'Be strong,' I whispered in his ear.

When he let go, he brushed his hand over mine, dropping the crystal into it. Gusta grabbed my other arm, pulling me away. I dropped the crystal into my pocket and looked back at my friend, before being jostled out of the chamber.

Chapter 14

Morning gongs sounded throughout the tunnels. I was facing an unknown fate, forced to leave my young friend behind to fend for himself, and all because Thani had woken early. I felt for the crystal in my pocket, the only solid thing I still owned, and stayed close at Gusta's heels.

Keeping a brisk pace, Gusta didn't speak as he led the way, through a network of familiar tunnels and beyond. We were climbing winding shallow slopes, until Gusta finally stopped next to a dark alcove. He reached for a torch and peered in, holding the light aloft.

'You first,' he said, bundling me through.

In the narrow space I saw steps dug into the rock, and with Gusta pushing from behind, I started to climb. The staircase coiled up a steep channel through the rocks, and with only torchlight to show the way, I climbed on all fours, keeping close to the wall. The higher we climbed, the air felt strangely fresh. Higher still and I saw we were approaching an archway. Light shone through the arch, not the orange glow of fire, but the bright white of daylight. It was a long time since I had seen the sun, and now I feared I was about to be thrown out of the mines; I had nowhere else to go.

'Go on,' Gusta said, when we reached the top, pushing me through the arch.

On the other side I was faced with a window, looking out across the desert view. The bright light hurt my eyes and I turned away, searching for the familiar darkness.

High in the mountains we were standing before a long corridor lined with wooden doors. At the far end of the corridor, a door opened and a woman came out. She appeared surprised to see us, although not as surprised as I was to see her. Aside from the fact I had no idea there were any women in the mountain, this woman was a strange sight. She appeared middle-aged, in her forties, maybe fifty, wearing a long red dress with a low scooped neck and ruffles hanging loosely over her shoulders; the bodice was pulled tight around her breasts, exaggerating her cleavage. Dressed up, while dishevelled at the same time, I'd never seen a woman look like her before. Long dark hair was piled on top of her head in an untidy bun, the make-up on her darkened eyes and red lips was smeared. As she walked towards us I saw her eyes were blood shot, and smelt the complex aroma of liquor and perfume mixed with smoke from the pipe she held in her hand. My eyes rested there, seeing the rings on her fingers were studded with crystals.

'Gusta?' she said. 'What are you doing here this early? And what have you brought him for?'

I was surprised by the confident tone she took, and the softly spoken way that Gusta responded.

'This one's been in the mines three years,' Gusta said. 'We've only just found out she's a girl.'

She glanced down at me, eyebrows raised, and bent down until her face was level with mine. Staring into my eyes, she raised the pipe to her lips and took a drag, breathing out a cloud of smoke in my face. I raised a hand to wipe my watering eyes.

'What's a girl doing in the mines?' she said, glancing up at Gusta.

'Beats me,' Gusta said.

She looked back at me and grabbed my chin. With her other hand she fumbled between my legs; I gasped when she squeezed.

'Are you untouched?' she said.

I stared at her, silent.

She let go and stood up to face Gusta.

'Well she looks a state, but that'll go down well,' she said. 'Okay, leave her with me.'

She leaned forward, brushing a kiss against Gusta's cheek, leaving behind a stain of red. He looked at me, a sly smile on his face, before he disappeared back into the stairwell.

The woman gripped my shoulders and led me down the corridor, where I saw girls' names scratched into the wood. She stopped at one door and opened it.

'You can have this room,' she said, ushering me inside.

I looked back at her as she stood, poised to leave. I wanted to ask what this place was, what I was doing here, but I knew better than to question my superiors. Even Gusta had spoken to her as though she was his equal.

'My name's Madam Isisa,' she said. 'I'll be back to get you later.'

She closed the door behind her, leaving me alone in this strange room.

I would never have believed such a lavish place existed had I not seen it with my own eyes. There was a bed draped in silk sheets and soft cushions, a dressing table littered with scent bottles, a lantern and decorative mirror, and a huge wardrobe, doors bulging open with dresses crammed inside. I looked around, not daring to touch anything, sure there must be some mistake. When a soft knocking sounded, I stared at the door, too afraid to speak. The knocking came again before the door slowly opened.

A young woman stood in the doorway, arms laden with a bowl of water, jug and towel. Wearing a tattered smock, an old rag tying back her hair, she looked at me, cautious at first before her eyes opened wide. I stared back, slowly remembering a face from the past.

'Ntombi?' I said; I could scarcely believe it.

She kicked the door closed behind her, and put the bowl down on the ground.

'I knew it must be you,' she said. 'A girl come up from the mines.'

She held her arms out, wrapping them around me. I stood, silent in her embrace, slowly folding my arms around her back. The gentleness of her touch brought tears to my eyes. I pressed my face into her hair; strong odours of smoke and grease were not what I remembered, but then so much had changed. Finally I pulled back to see her face; the vanquished spirit in her eyes was something I didn't recognise. She was not the same girl, but then neither was I.

'I can't believe you've been down there all this time,' she said. 'What have they done to you? You look so different.'

I reached up to feel my shaved head, and glanced cautiously at the mirror. I hadn't seen my own reflection since before the fire. Slowly I walked towards it: a stranger looked back. I reached up to touch my dark sunken eyes, cracked lips and hollow cheeks. It was a look I'd seen among the boys, but I'd never realised it to be my own.

I turned away from the mirror and looked back at Ntombi.

'What is this place?' I asked. 'What are *you* doing here?'

The door suddenly opened. Ntombi's face turned pale at the sight of Madam Isisa.

'What's been going on in here?' the Madam said, clipping Ntombi on the side of the head. 'Useless girl, get back to the kitchen.'

I stared after Ntombi as she scuttled out, head bent low, leaving me alone with the Madam.

'Get washed, and hurry up about it,' the Madam said, slamming the door closed. 'I can't have you seen looking like that.' I knelt down to wash my face and hands. 'And the rest, get those filthy rags off. There should be something here that fits you.'

I stood up to undress, glad to see the Madam turn her back as she rifled through the wardrobe. The crystal weighing heavy in my pocket, I kept one eye on the Madam as I bundled my clothes under the bed. After a thorough wash, Madam Isisa pulled an emerald green dress over my head, rearranging the neckline to create a cleavage I'd never seen on myself before.

'Not a bad fit,' she said, standing back. 'Not much we can do about a shaved head, but the girls will finish you off. Come on.'

I was taken to a room at the end of the hallway, filled with young women wearing colourful dresses. Some appeared as young as sixteen, others into their early twenties, chatting amicably as they styled each other's hair and applied make-up. One by one, quiet spread around the room as they saw me. I lowered my eyes, feeling foolish in the dress I wore, and intimidated at finding myself the object of attention.

'Calista,' the Madam said. 'See what you can do with her.'

A girl stepped forward, nodding and smiling at the Madam.

'Yes, Madam,' she said, and Madam Isisa turned and left.

When Calista turned to face me, her smile transformed into a smirk.

'I can't work miracles,' she said. 'They should send you back where you came from. You'll get no work up here, looking like that. You look like a boy in a dress.'

'Alright, Calista,' another young woman said. She came to me and put a hand on my shoulder. 'Don't look so nervous, we'll sort you out. I'm Fatma. Come, sit down.'

I was too surprised to speak, too confused to refuse, as she sat me at a table filled with combs and make-up. Other girls gathered round, all seeming friendly as they introduced themselves: Shula, Magda, Noka, Zola, Djamila…

'We've heard about you, working down in the mines,' Fatma said. 'No girl's ever been down there before.'

'I didn't know there were any girls here,' I said. 'What is this place?'

'The brothel,' Fatma said.

'Brothel?' I said. 'What's that?'

'You have been with a man, haven't you?' Shula asked.

'As if,' Calista said from across the room. 'Men don't want a flat chest and skinny arse! They want curves, not to mention hair.'

She flicked back her long dark hair, and rolled her hips to emphasize her point; the gesture brought laughter from the girls she was standing with.

'Take no notice,' Shula said. 'You can borrow my headscarf.'

She wound the scarf around my head, and then started on the make-up.

The girls' explanation only left me more confused, and anxious, but I was distracted by two women in the far corner of the room. I had gathered their names were Thando and Pamela, the only two not dressed and made-up. They kept to themselves, speaking only to each other, as Pamela stood stooped against the wall, chewing on some leaves. I wondered if she was ill. She was pale and sweating, rubbing her back as though in pain, while Thando was wiping her brow and giving her water to sip.

When Pamela started softly moaning, Thando said, 'I need to get her to her room. Cover for us.'

Magda opened the door a crack and peered out.

'It's clear,' she said.

When the two women left, I looked at Shula and asked, 'What's wrong with her? Is she sick?'

'She's not sick,' Shula said. 'She's pregnant.'

'She didn't look pregnant,' I said.

'Well, she's not showing yet,' Shula said. 'She needs to get rid of it before she does.'

'What do you mean, get rid of it?' I asked.

Shula sat down on the table to face me and asked, 'How old are you?'

It occurred to me that I couldn't be sure, although Gusta had said I'd been in the mines for three years.

'Nineteen?' I said, uncertain.

'Nineteen!' she said. 'Didn't your mother tell you about the facts of life? You get pregnant, you don't want the baby, you take a big dose of ogani leaves; it works every time. The men bring them in for us. Don't look so shocked. It's better that than the Madam finding out; she uses knitting needles; girls have bled to death that way.'

She was right, I was shocked. I had no idea what the Madam did with knitting needles but whatever it was, it sounded barbaric. I had never heard of ogani leaves before; monthly bleeds were as much as Mata had told me about becoming a woman. Anything I knew about boyfriends and girlfriends, and how women fell pregnant, was what I'd overheard. Now, among these young women, I realised just how naïve I was. Moreover, Mata had been burnt as a witch for dealing in herbal lore, and yet here of all places it was common practice. I kept my thoughts to myself and steeled my composure.

'Why didn't she want the baby?' I asked.

Shula said, 'In the brothel it doesn't matter if you want the baby or not. Here, the men aren't interested if you're with child. We all have to earn our keep.'

I was ignorant but I could follow the thread. As the afternoon passed, listening to the girls chat about who had lay with which miner, and who among the men paid well, I was left with no doubt as to the purpose of the brothel. In the mines I had lived by rigid rules; here I suspected was worse. More than forced manual labour for no apparent reward, in the brothel I feared I would have no control over my own body. I said little, just listened, hiding my nerves behind a fake smile, and thinking how I would find Ntombi the first chance I had.

Chapter 15

For all the sordid hints the girls had given, nothing could have prepared me for what I was about to enter.

Madam Isisa led the way through heavy wooden doors into a chamber of men, many I recognised from the mines. They were a raucous crowd, sitting around a huge table filled with bread, meats and jugs of ale; a feast compared to the insipid porridge served in the mines. It was a sickening sight to see the girls mingling around the room, kissed and groped and pulled to sit on men's knees. They seemed used to being man-handled by men twenty, thirty, forty years their senior, though when the Madam closed the doors behind us, it was apparent they had no choice.

The stuffy air, the heat from the fire burning in the hearth, I felt the walls close in around me. I stepped back against the wall, glanced at the door, desperate to leave. But Madam Isisa's sharp eyes were watching. She came to me and took hold of my shoulder.

'You will earn your keep here,' she said, pushing me into the crowd.

I clasped my arms around my waist, kept my gaze lowered to avoid anyone's eye, and pushed my way through the bodies, searching for a quiet corner out of sight of the Madam. Away from the table, on the far wall, an unoccupied stool was pushed into the alcove next to the fireplace. I went to it and sat down, inching my way back into the shadow. Head lowered, I kept a cautious eye on the room, daring to hope I might pass unnoticed. As time dragged, my back was aching and my buttocks turned numb, but I didn't dare move, fearful of drawing attention.

Ntombi's face in the crowd was a welcome sight. Dressed in the same tattered smock as before, her role as skivvy was clear as she carried trays of dishes to and from the table. Aside from the odd scowl as she was forced to push her way through, no one spoke or paid much attention to her at all. When she glanced in my direction, our eyes met. She turned back to the table, poured a ladle of stew into a bowl, and brought it to me.

'You should eat something,' she said in a low voice.

Eyes locked on hers, I felt the distance between us as I reached for the bowl, brushing my hand over hers. The man's hand seemed to come from nowhere, hitting Ntombi so hard on the side of her head it knocked her sideways. The bowl of stew splattered up the wall as she crumpled to the floor, cowering as the man towered over her.

'What are you doing mixing with whores?' he said, kicking her leg.

When he reached down, grabbing her by the hair, I stood up.

There was a warning look in her eyes as she silently mouthed at me, 'Don't.'

I held back, helpless as she was dragged across the room, watched by amused onlookers.

Seeing I had caught the eye of a young man, I sank back down into the shadows and stared at the ground. He came over regardless.

'Don't upset yourself,' he said. I was surprised by his gentle tone, and looked up at him. 'There's always trouble between those two; it's best you don't get involved. You'll only bring trouble for yourself.' He glanced at the wall, eyes lingering on the splatters of stew. 'I'll get you another bowl,' he said, 'and something to drink.'

I opened my mouth to refuse, but he turned his back and went to the table, returning with a fresh bowl of stew and a mug.

'I don't bite,' he said, with a smile that appeared kind as he offered the bowl.

'I'm not hungry,' I said, willing him to leave me alone.

He shrugged, put the bowl down on the ground, and said, 'A drink then?'

I was thirsty and, realising he wasn't going to leave, took the mug and sipped, instantly wincing at the bitter taste.

'You get used to the taste,' he said, still smiling. 'It looks like you found a quiet corner. Do you mind if I sit here? All that carrying on, it's not for me.'

He seemed different to the other men, genuine and kind. When I didn't answer, he pulled up a stool and sat down, leaning back against the wall.

He said his name was Khalid, and described the mines and brothel as 'a ruined place', claiming he'd never have come if he had known what it was really like. His words rang true and I listened as he talked long into the evening, distracted by Ntombi who reappeared to resume her serving duties. She didn't look at me again, and, troubled by the predicament, I sipped at the wine. Just as Khalid said, I got used to the taste and, despite myself, began to relax. He didn't attempt to touch me, just seemed glad to have someone to talk to. In return I found myself glad of his company, since it meant I was bothered by no other men. The sourness of the wine turned sweet and my thoughts foggy. When eventually I saw others leave, I yawned, longing to sleep. I stood up, but stumbled as the room appeared to tilt.

'Where are you going?' Khalid asked.

'To bed,' I said, struggling to straighten my line of vision. 'I need to lie down.'

'I'll walk with you.'

I wanted to tell him there was no need, but my focus was blurred and without his arm to hold onto, I couldn't walk straight. He held me up as I staggered down the hallway. By the time I found the right door, a strange nausea was washing over me in waves. When he opened the door I stumbled in, hitting my knees on the edge of the bed. I collapsed face down on the mattress and closed my eyes, but opened them again when I felt myself being rolled over onto my back. Khalid was there, kneeling over me.

'What are you doing?' I said, my words slurred.

His smile was gone. He didn't meet my eye as he untied the bodice of my dress. I tried to push his hands away but he grabbed my wrists, gripping them roughly above my head.

'Get off me,' I said, squirming as I tried to pull my hands free. But he was too strong.

He buried his face into my exposed breasts, flicking his tongue over my skin. I pushed up, lifting my head forward, and bit down on his cheek. As he cried out, momentarily losing his grip on my wrists, I pulled my hands free and hit out against his chest, trying to push him off. When he slapped me hard around the face, I tasted blood on my lip and lay back, stunned. He pushed my arms back over my head, gripped my wrists with one hand, and pulled the dress up to my waist. Then he pressed into me, jabbing me deep between my legs. I cried out in pain but he didn't stop, just slapped a hand over my mouth, stifling the sound. His thrusts came hard and fast, sounding with a knocking as the bed banged against the wall. I closed my eyes, helpless, until finally he slipped from my body. He left without a word. For a while I lay staring at the door, confused. My stomach lurched and I rolled onto my side, hanging my head over the side of the bed and vomiting on the floor. Stomach empty, I pulled the sheets tight around me and stared hopelessly into the darkness.

I awoke the next morning, feeling my mouth dry and head pounding. My lip was swollen and I brushed against it with my tongue, tasting dried blood. I stared at the ceiling in confusion, smelling stale vomit. Slowly I recalled the night before, reaching down to feel a damp patch between my legs. I looked at my fingers, covered in blood, and curled myself into a ball, forehead pressed against the cold hard wall.

A gentle knocking sounded at the door, before it opened a crack.

A voice whispered, 'Suni? Are you alone?'

'Ntombi?' I said. 'Is that you?'

She came in carrying a tray, and closed the door behind her. I watched her put the tray on the table, saw her bruised cheek and swollen eye, and pushed myself up to lean on my elbow. She glanced down at the pool of vomit on the floor and at the bloodstained sheet.

'I'll bring some soap and water,' she said.

'Don't go,' I said, reaching for her hand.

She brushed the tips of my fingers and said, 'I'll come straight back.' She turned to the table and poured a mug of water, handing it to me. 'Drink this,' she said. 'It'll help you feel better.'

I sipped from the mug, until she returned soon after with a bowl of soapy water. She pulled the soiled sheet out from under me, and then set to work scrubbing the floor. I tried to stand, wanting to help, but I felt nauseous, my legs shaking. I sat back down, watching her clean up after me, ashamed of what had happened and embarrassed that Ntombi knew.

She finished cleaning and brought the tray to the bed, pouring more water and handing me a hunk of bread.

'Eat,' she said. 'It'll help settle your stomach.'

I took a bite, feeling a tear roll down my cheek as I chewed. She brushed it away, her soft fingers lingering on my swollen mouth.

'Don't fight them, Suni,' she said, sitting down next to me. 'They won't hit if you don't fight them.'

I looked at her, reached up to touch her face, tracing a finger under her bruised eye.

'How can you stand it?' I said. 'How can any woman here stand it?'

'It's different for me,' she said. 'Wiseman's my husband.'

'You're married!'

She lowered her eyes and said, 'He doesn't always hit me. Sometimes he even sticks up for me with the Madam. It's just when he's had a drink and he doesn't know what he's doing.'

I remembered the girl I had once known, proud, strong and resilient. Now I saw only a young woman beaten by life. We were both battered and bruised. I put the bread back on the tray, feeling queasy.

'Why do I feel so ill?' I said.

'You drank too much wine,' she said, handing me the mug. 'Drink some more water.'

My hand was shaking but she kept it steady, as I raised the mug to my lips and sipped.

'I'll never drink wine again,' I said. 'Why does anyone drink it when it makes you so sick?'

'I think the women drink to forget,' she said. 'Girls soon get used to the taste.'

I put the mug back on the tray and reached for Ntombi's hand.

'How did you end up here?' I asked.

'Wiseman got a job here after we were married, and brought me with him.'

'How did you meet him?' I asked.

'He used to come to the bakery,' she said. 'And, one day, he started paying me attention. Maybe it's stupid, but I liked it. Apart from you, hardly anyone ever spoke to me. He was charming and kind; I couldn't believe it when he proposed. Life had been so hard for so long, and here he was, a man promising to take care of me.' She paused, looking into space; her eyes narrowed as though confused. 'I try to be a good wife; he's not all bad.'

A thought slowly dawned. 'What happened to Wanda?'

She shook her head, still staring into space.

'Ntombi?'

Her eyes met mine as she said, 'Wiseman said he'd look after him. He promised me. But when we got here, he had him sent down to the mines. Sometimes he lets him visit, but he always sends him back.'

Struck with the realisation, I said, 'I was with him. Wanda was brought to my chamber.'

She squeezed my hand. 'I'm glad he had you.'

'But he's got no one now. And it's not safe down there: there are roof collapses, even in the main tunnels.'

'I know,' she said. 'Wiseman enjoys telling me stories of boys buried alive.'

'We have to get Wanda up here,' I said. 'And then we have to leave.'

She shook her head, eyebrows gently narrowed as she said, 'Suni, you're not thinking straight. There is no way out of here. You can't just leave.'

But that was not something I could accept.

Chapter 16

I received a slap on the side of the head from the Madam when I told her I was ill and needed to stay in bed. She told me I wasn't ill, just lazy, as she sent me down to prepare for the men. None of the girls mentioned my split lip, just diligently covered it with powder. The sight of Pamela in the dining chamber was distraction from my own angst. Despite being sore from ending the pregnancy the day before, still she was forced to 'entertain'.

I skirted around the edge of the room, keeping a distance from the table where people congregated, determined to go to bed alone when the doors finally opened. But before long, for all my efforts, I found myself face to face with Gusta.

Later that night, while Gusta was sleeping in my bed, I sat on the cold hard floor, knees tight to my chest as I rocked to and fro. Eyes on my pile of clothes hidden beneath the bed, I thought of my crystal. I longed to hold it, to travel to the world of mist and see my mother there. It was so close, but as long as I was in the brothel it would never be safe to look into the crystal again. I turned my gaze to the door. The hallway outside was quiet; it was a long time since I'd heard anyone walk by. I stood up and gently prodded Gusta's arm; he didn't stir. I crept to the door and opened it ajar, peering out into the hallway. Seeing no one around, I stole down to the dining chamber in search of Ntombi.

The table was piled with clean crockery; apart from embers glowing in the hearth all traces of the evening's debauchery were gone. I crept over to the archway and peered into the kitchen, hearing snoring coming from an adjoining chamber on the far side.

'Ntombi,' I whispered.

She didn't answer. I crept into the dark room, ducking under pots and pans hanging from the ceiling as I whispered her name. My foot knocked against a stool. I reached down to stop it from falling, my heart racing as the stool scraped loudly on the stone ground. Hearing movement from the adjoining chamber I ducked down under the table, listening to padding footsteps cross the kitchen. I was relieved to see Ntombi's silhouette standing in the dim light of the archway. With the sound of unbroken snoring, I crept out of my hiding place.

Ntombi watched me emerge with wide eyes, grabbed my hand and led me over to the fireplace.

'What are you doing here?' she whispered. 'You have to go back to your room.'

'I can't go back to that,' I said, stepping closer and dropping my head to rest in the nape of her neck.

'You have to,' she said, stroking my hair. 'If Wiseman catches you here...'

I raised my head to face her and said, 'There has to be a way out of here.'

'There isn't,' she said, 'only the gateway to the mines and they keep that guarded.'

'This place is a prison,' I said. 'No one talks about life outside; no one talks about leaving.'

'You have to make the best of it, Suni. What else can we do?'

'Where do the girls even come from?' I asked. 'How did they get here?'

'Most of them were sold by their fathers,' she said.

'Their fathers!'

'Keep your voice down.'

'Why would any father send his daughter to be used by men?' I whispered.

'It's not all bad,' she said. 'Some girls do get out.'

'How?'

85

'Taken by a man to be their mistress,' she said. 'There was a girl a while back, had her release paid for, set up in a house in town.'

I felt numb.

'Ntombi! Who are you talking to?'

Hearing Wiseman's voice, we stared at each other in fright.

'No one,' Ntombi called back. 'Just myself.'

'Mad bitch, get back here.'

We hugged briefly before we went our separate ways.

Days passed, men came and went, and with each encounter my heart grew harder. The brief times I could be alone with Ntombi was my only solace in this oppressive world: she at least saw me as more than a whore. I found little comfort from the other girls; their apparent acceptance at being treated as mere objects was disturbing, until I discovered some had been in the brothel for over five years. They were survivors, but survival came at a high price.

I refused to accept being a prisoner of the brothel would be my fate, refused to accept that the only route to freedom was to sell myself completely. It was for more than myself, it was for the quest to restore the Mantra. Each day as I dressed for the evening, I glanced under my bed, at the pile of clothes concealing my crystal. The thought that I had a secret was a comfort, the one thing that the men couldn't touch. I never lost hope that I would one day look into it again; I had to. That was the only thing that had kept my spirits strong all the long years in the mines, and it was not something I was willing to let go of.

Then, one evening, hope presented itself.

A man was watching me from across the table, no one I recalled having seen before. He stood out from the rest: his clothes untidy, hair and beard unkempt. I tried to keep my distance but his eyes were fixed on me, until finally he approached.

He didn't speak at first, just stood in my way, a strange, confused look on his face before eventually he said, 'I need to talk to you.'

We were taught to be submissive, but this man was making me feel more uneasy than usual.

'So talk,' I said.

'Not here. In your room.'

I didn't want to be alone with this man; I didn't want to be alone with any man, but with the Madam watching I led the way.

I edged away, wary, as he closed the door behind us.

'You said you just wanted to talk,' I said.

He slowly turned and met my eye, as he said, 'It is you, isn't it?'

'What?'

'Mata's daughter. My daughter.'

I felt like I was sinking.

He stepped closer and said, 'I knew it the moment I saw you.'

I shook my head and stepped back, staring at his face, seeing features resembling my own: the tone of his skin and line of his jaw. *Mata.* It was a name I'd not heard spoken in so long.

Voice cracked, I said, 'I looked for you. And this is where I find you...' I held my hands up to my face. 'I don't believe this.'

Seeing shame on his face, in that moment I despised him. This was the man who had broken Mata's heart, and he was not worthy.

'I know this is hard,' he said. 'Just give me a chance. Tell me your name.'

'Hard! You don't even know my name. You left us, for this... Mata tried to tell me to forget about you, but I had some stupid idea you might be a good man. But you're not, you're just like the rest.'

Tears were spilling down my cheeks. Angrily I wiped them away.

He stood still, impotent, and asked, 'Where is your mother?'

'Dead,' I said. 'Murdered. It's why I came looking for you.'

For a moment he stared at me speechless, before he hung his head. Arms clutched around his waist as though in pain, he sank down on the edge of the bed.

'I tried to tell her to stop,' he said. 'I told her one day she'd get herself killed. I didn't want to leave her, I didn't want to leave either of you, but she wouldn't stop.'

My legs felt weak and I crouched down on the ground. I wanted to blame him, but I too had been afraid Mata was in too deep.

'You never came to see me,' I said.

'I know,' he said, voice filled with misery. 'I'm sorry. I came here hoping to prove to Mata that there was another way. I was wrong.'

I pressed my knuckles into the ground, arms taut.

'So this is what you do,' I said, 'use women like me.' I didn't try to hide my contempt. 'I wouldn't be here if it wasn't for you.'

'I'm sorry,' he said, staring down at the ground.

'Is that it?' I said, leaning forward. 'Is that all you can say! Look at me! Or can't you look at me? Am I just a whore to you?'

He slowly raised his eyes to look at me, wary. 'Don't say that,' he quietly said.

I saw the shame on his face, felt my own shame, and looked down at the cold hard floor to hide fresh tears welling in my eyes.

Moments passed before he finally said, 'I'll get you out of here.'

I looked up, sinking back to rest on my ankles. 'How?'

'I'll tell people you're my mistress, and move you into a house in town.'

'No!'

'It's the only way. No one knows I'm your father and we need to keep it that way, for both our sakes.'

He would deny me, after everything I'd been through. I hated him for that. But I knew he was right. He wasn't strong, he held no sway here, no one man did; my time in the mountains had taught me that. The King was all powerful and the mines served the King; the whole land served the King. It dawned on me I had nowhere to go.

'I can't go back to town,' I said. 'I'd be recognised.'

He rubbed his chin, eyes narrowed as he slowly stood. I felt the silence stretch out between us.

Finally he said, 'Maybe there's another way.'

'What?'

He paced the length of the room and back, and said, 'I don't know, it's dangerous.'

'What is?' I stood up to face him.

'I know of people you'd be safe with,' he said. 'Your mother's people.'

'What are you talking about?'

'The resistance,' he said. 'When the King took power, they fled into the valley beyond these mountains.'

I shook my head and said, 'The resistance were all killed.'

'No, that's just a lie the King spread. He wanted people to believe he'd crushed the enemy, crushed hope. The fact the resistance survived is the biggest threat this regime faces.'

I thought of the men in the mines, the town guards, the palace guards. As courageous as my great grandmother had been, as the resistance had been, it was hard to imagine how they had survived, how they continued to survive.

'But if they're just in the valley beyond the mountains, how are they safe from the King's men?' I asked.

'Because they're protected. A strange mist lies low over the mountain summits; it's said to be haunted. Years ago an entire army attempted to cross, to kill the last of the traitors. Only one man made it back; blabbering about ghosts and spells, apparently he was never the same since.' His eyes narrowed as he continued. 'Every so often men get sent to check out the path. None of them have been seen since. Like I said, it's dangerous.'

Dangerous or not, the thought of people, my people, living free of the King's tyranny, was more than I could have hoped for.

'Do you know the way?' I asked.

He nodded and said, 'First I want to know my daughter's name.'

'My name is Suni.'

I memorized all he said, a route that began with the chimney in the dining chamber.

'You should leave soon,' he said. 'The weather's still fair up there, but the cold will be setting in soon. I'll go to town tomorrow, get some supplies, and be back the day after.'

'I won't be going alone,' I said.

I thought I saw a spark of hope in his eyes, but he had chosen the mines once, and probably would again. I didn't even know if I wanted him to come.

'I'm taking two others,' I said. 'Ntombi, the server; and her nephew, Wanda. Wanda's down in the mines; you'll have to make sure he's brought up here. I'll speak to Ntombi in the morning.'

He nodded and said, 'Looks like you'll be needing more shoes.'

I let slip my first smile for my father.

Chapter 17

The next morning I stood with an ear pressed against the door, listening for Ntombi. Finally I heard quiet footsteps and the soft splash of water. I opened the door and hurried her inside, waiting for her to set the bowl of water on the floor. When she stood up to face me, I saw a fresh bruise on her cheek.

I held both her hands in mine and said, 'Just two more days and Wiseman will never be able to hurt you again.'

'What are you talking about?' she said.

'We're getting out of here, tomorrow night; you, me and Wanda.'

She frowned and shook her head.

'You have to stop this, Suni. Hoping for the impossible, you're just making it worse for yourself. You need to accept things the way they are.'

She tried to pull her hands away but I held them tightly and said, 'Ntombi, listen to me. I met my father last night. He's getting us out of here.'

As I told of the escape, and the people we were to join in the valley, Ntombi's surprise turned to confusion.

'Wiseman would kill me before he let me leave,' she said.

I tucked a stray lock of hair behind her ear and said, 'You'll be long gone before Wiseman realises.'

She managed a smile that spoke of her gratitude.

The thought of leaving any girl behind left me plagued with guilt, but their loyalties were unclear. Ntombi was the only one I could trust.

In the girls' company I said as little as possible, as they chatted excitedly, firing questions about Fazi. He had spread the rumour that I was his mistress, distasteful but it served me well: being 'out of bounds' kept other men away.

The following evening, entering the dining chamber, I discretely searched among the faces around the table looking for Fazi. He wasn't there. Nearing the kitchen I saw Wanda, peering out from behind the archway. His glance drifted past me without recognition as he watched the sordid gathering. I wanted to go to him, to shield him, but I was afraid, up close, he might recognise me. I looked around the room, searching for Ntombi, intending to ask her to move Wanda out of sight.

She was at the far end of the table, piling a batch of bread rolls, head turned, distracted by something in the corner of the room. I went closer to try to catch her eye, but she was gazing intently at Wiseman, sitting with Zola on his lap, his face buried in her cleavage. Bullied and abused by her husband, I had assumed Ntombi hated Wiseman. Seeing her now, watching him with another woman, I realised I had been wrong. She was frowning, eyes and mouth in thin lines as though jealous, as she grabbed a stack of dirty dishes and made for the kitchen.

I followed and saw her crash into Wanda, dropping the dishes.

'Look what you've done now!' she shouted at him. She bent down, grabbing him by the arms and shaking him roughly. 'I told you not to get in the way.'

Wanda cowered, silent, as she cleared up the mess. When she disappeared into the kitchen, he sank back against the wall, eyes wide and staring.

I thought back to the day I'd first met Wanda, alone in the shack with only wild dogs for company. Ntombi had been just a girl then, struggling to survive. I'd never seen her angry before, would never have believed she could hurt Wanda. All the times he had returned to the mines with bruises, seeing Wiseman attack Ntombi I had assumed it was him; now I wasn't so sure. She was beaten and bullied by her husband, and yet she had feelings for him, enough to make her jealous and angry. I thought I knew who she was, but this was a situation more complicated than I could understand.

Wiseman walked past, heading for the kitchen.

'What are you doing out here?' he said to Wanda, kicking him in the leg as he walked by.

Eyes on Wanda I started towards him, but was stopped by a hand on my arm. It was Fazi.

'Wait,' he said. 'You'll ruin it. I'll go.'

He fetched a pitcher of wine and two mugs, and took them to Wiseman in the kitchen. I watched them drink together, as Fazi kept Wiseman talking and refilling his mug. After the third mug Wiseman stumbled, collapsing against the table. Fazi grabbed his arm, pulling it across his shoulders as he half carried Wiseman to bed.

Fazi came back to me and said, 'It'll be a while before he wakes up.'

'What did you do?' I asked.

'Sleeping potion in his wine. He's dead to the world.'

The evening dragged. Wanda fell asleep still propped against the cold wall, while Ntombi worked hard serving the table, offering her nephew only a fleeting glance. When finally the drunken party left, I ran to my room and ripped off the dress. Unravelling the scarf tied around my head, I paused, thinking of Shula. My friendships with the women were founded on circumstance, and, for my part, had been lacking in truth; still I had grown fond of them. I folded the scarf and placed it neatly on the bed, then dressed in my old clothes. I took the crystal out of the pocket, pausing to feel its rough edges before tucking it safely in the hem. Then I grabbed the sack Fazi had left for me and left that hateful room for the last time.

Ntombi was busy damping down the fire while Fazi stood idly by. Wanda was still sleeping and I went to him, crouching down beside him and gently stroking his hair. He woke quickly, a startled look in his eyes.

'It's okay, Wanda,' I said, smiling. 'It's me.'

He reached up to touch the hair that had grown on my head.

I held out my hand and said, 'Come. We're leaving here. We're going to a safe place.'

He took my hand and followed to the fireplace, where I emptied the sack, dividing out the capes and shoes. Ntombi went to pull a cape over Wanda's head, handing it to me when he backed away from her. I dressed Wanda, and myself, then looked at Ntombi, seeing she had made no move to do the same.

'Ntombi, come on,' I said, pushing the shoes towards her.

She hesitated before pulling them on.

Fazi said, 'Once you get to the top, head south. Your path is between two tall peaks; you can't miss them. When you're on the path just keep moving forward. Some say the mist is a spell to trap trespassers, others say it's haunted. Just keep going, and don't listen to the voices.'

I nodded. Compared to the brothel, I was not afraid of ghosts.

Fazi put his hand on my shoulder and said, 'You should get going.'

I nodded and offered an awkward smile; he was my father, but there was so little history between us.

'Ntombi!' Hearing Wiseman's yell we stared at one another in fright. 'Where are you? Get here!'

I pushed Wanda into the fireplace and scrambled in after.

'Coming!' Ntombi answered.

I turned to see her kick off the shoes.

'What are you doing?' I whispered. 'Come on.'

She shook her head and backed away.

'Take Wanda and go!' she said.

I felt torn, watching her run across the chamber and disappear into the kitchen.

'You have to go, Suni,' Fazi said.

I looked down at Wanda. Seeing his frightened face, I lifted him into the chimney and climbed up after.

Chapter 18

It was a long, awkward climb, scrambling around for footholds, pushing Wanda up through thick soot. Finally we emerged out into the open, breathing fresh air. My skin tingled with the feel of it, cool and crisp. After years locked in the confines of the mountain, the vast, moon-drenched landscape was overwhelming. I looked back down the chimney with regret, thinking of Ntombi still trapped.

Wanda huddled against my legs. Sadness at leaving Ntombi was overshadowed by the need to get us both to safety. I wiped the soot from his face and pulled up his hood.

'We have to walk now, Wanda,' I said. 'It might be a long way, but I'll help you.'

He simply nodded. I smiled and took his hand, inspired by the courage of someone so young.

The summit appeared like a giant bowl, flat rock edged by a ridge. Beyond the ridge, to the south, just as Fazi had said, two tall peaks disappeared into the night sky. I kept my eyes fixed on them as I led Wanda on; somewhere beyond those peaks lived my mother's people, my people.

The ground was loose slate that crunched underfoot, in places cracked into gullies. Forced to weave around, it was a slow trek to the ridge, and Wanda was sleeping in my arms long before we arrived. Up close I saw the ridge was higher than I had thought. Arms and legs aching, I looked back, needing to rest. Nothing stirred. I climbed up to a boulder and lay Wanda down, curling in beside him. I didn't plan on sleep, but my eyes felt heavy, and before long I sank into a dream.

It was a busy day at market; crowds of people jostled between stalls carrying baskets brimming with fruit, vegetables, beans and spices. I was there in the crowd, among familiar sights, but every other sense told me I didn't belong. Spiced coffee was being poured, over-ripe fruit that should smell sweet was attracting flies, but there was no aroma in the air. People were talking all around me, some right next to me, but their voices sounded distant. I looked at their sweaty faces, saw the afternoon sun, but I was cold.

I felt a jolt from behind; the short, sharp sensation of heat meeting cold. I turned to see a man walk by, seemingly oblivious to the fact he had just walked into me. *You don't belong.* A boy brushed against my arm as he walked past; I saw his arm move through mine, felt the shock of the encounter, the shock of realising I was a mere apparition in a solid world.

I glimpsed my stall through the crowd, and saw my mother busy at her loom. I made my way towards her, saw people look right through me as I side-stepped around them. *You don't belong.* As I approached, Mata looked up and waved. I went to wave back, but realised she was looking past me. I turned and saw myself, as I was when I was younger, waving at Mata. Another shock came from behind, different from the rest; it felt like cold meeting cold. I turned and saw Mata's apparition look straight at me, smiling.

I opened my eyes to see Wanda looking down at me. He moved aside and I cupped a hand to my brow, dazzled by the morning sun. Still feeling the cold of the dream, I pulled the cape in tight around me as I sat up. The dream had left me with a sense of longing, and I felt for the crystal, reassured by the thought I would soon be safe to look into it again.

After a ration of bread and water, we made a slow climb up the ridge, weaving around boulders and patches of loose shale. We looked out over the top, seeing a clear view of the two peaks; the pathway between was dark and narrow, barely a crack. I hesitated, doubtful of the way ahead, and heard sharp, shrill cries carried on a southerly breeze. A bird came soaring between the two splintering summits on a course towards us. We both stared in awe as it circled over our heads, watched its huge wings glide effortlessly on the current.

'I think it's an eagle,' I said, casting my mind back to childhood memories of Mata's stories. Eagles hadn't been sighted on this barren land since before the King.

It broke from circling, flying back against the breeze. Such a magical sight, watching it disappear back between the peaks, listening to its echoing cries fade into the distance, I imagined it to have been a sign. I squeezed Wanda's hand as we scrambled down the ridge, heading for the pathway.

In the shadow of the peaks the air turned cool, cooler still when we entered the pathway with an overhang eclipsing the sun. I clung to Wanda's hand as I led the way, forced into single file as the walls were tight around us. In places we had to squeeze ourselves between the sheer faces either side. I was beginning to fear that Fazi had been mistaken, and that we were heading to a dead end. But the path gradually widened, and, feeling the sun on my skin again, I looked up to see the sky, amazed by the sight of a white cloud drift overhead; clear blue sky was all I had ever known.

The sun shone down but the air grew colder. Rounding a corner the ground was hidden by mist, ankle-deep. I pulled Wanda closer to me as we went ahead, cool mist creeping up our legs until it reached my knees. I clutched the cape tighter at my throat, seeing my breath like clouds of white vapour rising out of my mouth. The further we went the mist grew deeper, until Wanda was fully immersed. I kept tight hold of his hand and reached for the wall to guide me, as mist crept up over my chest and head.

The misty haze was blinding. I kept my hand in contact with the wall, slowly feeling the way forward. There was a sound in the air, faint at first but growing louder, until murmuring voices surrounded us. Wanda was pulling on my hand.

I bent down and whispered in his ear, 'Don't be afraid.'

I tried to heed my own words, as I stood up straight and clenched my jaw, sure that the mournful, whispering chorus were not the voices of the living. I took a step forward, and another, remembering Fazi's warning not to listen to the voices. I reached for the wall, determined. My fingers searched, but they touched only air.

Disorientated, I reached for Wanda, bringing him in front and clutching his shoulders, walking slowly forwards. I imagined the voices were trying to ensnare us, and, with no markers to guide the way, I focused my thoughts on my crystal. Many nights I had explored the misty world it concealed, without fear; there was nothing to fear. The ghosts that roamed there never harmed me, my own mother was among them. I propelled us on, telling myself that the cool mist brushing against my skin was familiar.

I stumbled when Wanda suddenly dropped to the ground. I crouched down, feeling for his arms, trying to pull him to his feet, but he was hanging like a dead weight.

'Wanda, come on, stand up,' I said.

He showed no signs of response, his body limp.

I picked him up, cradling him in my arms as I clutched him to my chest. Not knowing whether I was going in the right direction, I walked forwards, desperate to be free of the mist. The ground was sloping gently downwards, as smooth rock turned to rough gravel. I inched forward, feeling with my feet ahead of each step, feeling something prickly brushing against my ankles. The mist was slowly clearing, revealing patches of green grass on the path. We emerged from the peaks onto a mountainous slope, looking out over a sweeping view of the valley.

I gazed out over lush green grasslands; a sight so unbelievable it brought tears to my eyes. Such a sharp contrast to the barren land on the other side of the mountains, it hardly seemed possible.

'We made it,' I said, slowly lowering my eyes to look down at Wanda.

Sight of his face was a shock; his eyes were closed, skin pale and lips tinged blue. I dropped to my knees, fearing he was dead.

'Wanda?' I said, my hand hovering over his face.

I gently patted his cheek, confused and relieved to feel his skin felt hot. I put an ear to his chest, and felt the rise and fall of slow breaths.

'Wanda, wake up,' I said, gently shaking his shoulders, but he didn't stir.

I lifted back his eyelids, saw his eyes rolled back in his head; it wasn't anything I'd seen before. I looked back at the mist, wondering what evil lurked there, and turned back to Wanda, scooping him into my arms. Desperate to get away from the mist, desperate to find help, I scrambled down the steep slopes. I was alone, with no idea how to save my friend.

Traipsing over the foothills I saw no sign of human habitation in this green wilderness. The valley was vast, and any naïve notion that a community of people would be waiting to welcome us, was replaced by despair. My arms ached from carrying Wanda, my legs were weary. When I could go no further, I sank to my knees and lay Wanda down in the grass. All we had survived, the distance we had come, but it felt in vain. I rested my head on Wanda's chest and cried.

Chapter 19

I was startled by a hand gently shaking my shoulder.

'Who are you?' a man's voice said.

I looked up and saw a man peering out from the hood of a cape. Fright turned to relief at the sight of his dark weathered skin, an appearance quite unlike the ashen faces of the men in the mountains. Thinking we had been found by the resistance, I glanced around for others, but the man was alone, and unarmed.

'Can you help him?' I asked, moving aside to show Wanda.

Eyes fixed on Wanda, he crouched down next to him. There was maturity in the stranger's solid stature and confidence with which he examined Wanda, but judging by his face, I considered he wasn't much older than me. He pressed a hand on Wanda's brow, gently lifted his eyelids and parted his lips, felt down along each arm, across his chest and down his torso with the skill of a healer. His hands gently patted down Wanda's side until he stopped, and pulled out a feather-bound dart.

'What is that?' I asked.

'A poison dart,' he said, carefully wrapping it in a wadding of cloth and putting it in his pocket.

'Poison!' I said.

'The boy's dying, but there might still be time.' He scooped Wanda into his arms and stood up. 'Come, follow me.'

The stranger appeared at home in the wilderness as did the eagle in the vast skies, as he hurried over the foothills. At the rise of one hill we came to a sheer drop. The man shifted Wanda to drape him over his shoulder, while he climbed down to the overhang below. I followed after, arriving at the entrance to a cave, with a burnt-out fireplace, pots littering the ground, and bundles of leaves and twigs hanging from the roof.

The man laid Wanda down inside the cave, and piled dry grasses in the stone fireplace.

'Cover him,' he said, striking a flint over the grasses that were soon smouldering. 'We need to keep him warm.'

I went to a pile of blankets in the corner, seeing, up close, they were animal skins mottled with different shades and markings. I lay one over Wanda and sat down next to him, wiping his sweat-drenched brow with the sleeve of my cape and feeling his skin hot to the touch.

'He's burning up,' I said.

'We need to get the fever out,' the man said, adding twigs to the fire.

He set a pot of water to boil, adding a bouquet of unfamiliar leaves and stirring it until it simmered. He poured a bowl and handed it to me.

'Drink it,' he said. 'It will refresh you.'

I sniffed the tea but didn't recognise the aroma; a faint whiff of mint was overpowered by something pungent. Trusting in the stranger, I took a sip; it tasted better than it smelt.

A curious collection of roots and dried fungi were added to the pot, nothing I recognised. He lifted the pot aside to cool, and pounded seeds into a pulp. When he lifted Wanda's shirt, I was shocked to see an open wound, red and inflamed.

'It looks like its festering,' I said.

'We need to get the poison out,' the man said, smearing pulp over the wound.

'Where did the dart come from?' I asked.

'One of the keepers. He's lucky; not many of them use darts.'

'Keepers?' I asked.

'They guard the mist, protecting the valley.' He paused to look at me, eyes gently narrowed. 'I've never known anyone get past them before.'

I lowered my eyes, confused by the suspicion in his voice.

With a thick layer of pulp daubed over Wanda's wound, the stranger covered it with cloth and then returned to the pot, pouring a bowl of cool tea. Wanda's eyes were still closed but the stranger gently parted his lips, patiently teasing drops of the tea into Wanda's mouth. I watched, relieved to see a healthy shade return to Wanda's cheeks.

'It'll take time,' the man said, putting the bowl aside. 'But I think he'll recover.'

He turned back to tend to the fire, gaze fixed as he stoked the flames. The silence between us felt uneasy.

Finally, I asked, 'What's your name?'

'Juna,' he said. After a long pause, he turned to face me, eyebrows furrowed as he said, 'You came by a dangerous path. The spell the elders weave brings a fog no one but the keepers can see through. People here believe all outsiders are spies for the King. You shouldn't have come.'

'We're not spies,' I said, feeling my skin prickle and my cheeks grow warm. 'My name is Suni, and the King is my enemy. His men murdered my mother for treason. We came looking for believers of the Mantra; my mother's people. We've got no-where else to go.'

'Is the boy your brother?' he asked.

'Wanda's my companion,' I said.

I didn't want to speak of the dark world inside the mountains, and was relieved when he didn't question me further. He rubbed a hand across his mouth as he glanced down at Wanda, then stood up and fetched a catapult from the far corner.

'I'm going hunting,' he said. 'Keep the boy warm while I'm gone. He needs rest; you can stay here tonight.'

I watched him leave, anxious by the lack of reassurance. One night, and then what? Hearing Wanda softly whimper I looked down at him. His eyes were still closed but his mouth gently parted as he softly moaned. It was a relief just to see some response. I felt his forehead; his skin felt clammy and cool. I pulled another blanket over him and stoked the fire, every so often checking his temperature. Violent tremors came suddenly, his whole body shaking. I felt helpless watching his eyes squeezed shut and jaw clenched, as though he was in pain.

'Ssh,' I soothed, wiping the sweat soaking his skin.

Time dragged while Wanda suffered a fitful fever, but with his hand gripped in mine, slowly I felt the shivers subside. Still I kept my eyes fixed on the cave entrance, willing Juna to return. Finally he did, with a dead creature slung over his shoulder; with long ears and muscular legs, I wondered if it was a hare.

He knelt down next to Wanda, felt his brow, and said, 'He's over the worst. He'll need meat when he wakes.'

He lay the creature down next to the fire and deftly skinned, diced and added it to a pot of water. Adding herbs he cooked up an aromatic broth, the meat so tender it fell off the bone. By the time a bowlful was served, Wanda's eyes had opened.

From the first, Wanda appeared relaxed with Juna; an instant trust that was curious to see. I watched the readiness in which Wanda accepted each spoonful Juna offered, the care and patience Juna took while feeding a sickly boy, and the tenderness he showed when stroking Wanda's hair, telling him to rest. When Wanda closed his eyes, the stranger poured another bowl and handed it to me. He afforded me only a fleeting glance, before he turned away, served himself a bowl, and retreated to the mouth of the cave looking out.

'Is this your home?' I asked.

'Just a place I stay when I'm tracking deer,' he said, chewing a mouthful of meat.

The thought of deer, hare and eagles was intriguing, but he still hadn't said we could stay beyond a night.

'Do you live far from here?' I asked. When he didn't answer, I added, 'It's just, apart from your cave, I haven't seen signs that anyone lives here.'

He put the spoon down in the bowl and lowered his hands, gazing silently out over the view before he finally said, 'You'll need to speak to the elders, but it's too far for the boy to travel. I'll take you to my home in the morning; you can stay until he's well enough to go on.'

It was a reluctant invitation from a solitary man, a healer who could not turn his back on an injured soul. Wanda trusted him, a boy whose judgement I trusted. And so our lives had become entwined. As darkness fell and I lay down to sleep, I thought of a community led by elders. Juna may have chosen a solitary life, but I was yearning to belong.

Chapter 20

Night brought a strange chorus. While Juna and Wanda slept, I crept to the mouth of the cave and looked out. The sights and sounds brought Mata's stories of old to life: low-pitched buzzing; grass rustling; and intermittent chirping from down below, I wondered if it came from crickets. The air was flickering with the lights of fireflies, and on the ground below, yellow eyes were watching. When one and then another started to howl, there was no mistaking the sound of wolves.

Mesmerized, I watched and listened. At the break of dawn the wolves moved on, and a herd of deer arrived to graze; every so often they raised their heads with ears pricked, alert.

'They can smell the wolves,' Juna said. I looked round to see him standing behind me, his arms loosely folded, his face relaxed as he gazed at the deer. 'Red deer; small but quick. An adult will outrun a wolf, but the young are easy targets.'

'I grew up believing the Mantra had left this land,' I said, turning back to face the view. 'But seeing all this wildlife, and clouds in the sky, maybe it's still here, for this valley at least.'

'I imagine it does look like that to you, coming from the desert,' he said. 'But this valley's not what it once was; the elders weave their spells but the rainy season gets shorter each year.'

I wanted to ask more about the mysterious elders and a mist woven from spells, but hearing Wanda stirring, I followed Juna back into the cave.

After finishing the broth from the night before, Juna lifted Wanda onto his back and climbed down from the cave. The herd of deer had moved on, leaving only tracks in the grass; still Wanda looked around with wonder in his eyes, at the sight of rolling grassland and wild flowers. We had only crossed mountains but for the difference, it was as though we had travelled to distant lands far across the sea.

Two birds came flying overhead, landing on a curious tree with branches spiked with woody thorns and fringed with clusters of tiny leaves. It appeared an impenetrable mass of twigs surrounding the nest in the centre, but the birds negotiated the lethal looking barbs with ease. Once safely in their nest they sang a shrill song that to me sounded magical. It was hard to believe this hidden valley was not touched by the Mantra; I wondered if it was the power of the elders that kept the rains coming.

The mountain foothills met with stretching plains, predominantly flatland but every so often marked by small hills. Juna's home was the first and only dwelling we saw, a rustic cottage standing in the shadow of a hillside. From a distance it appeared as though random pieces of wood surrounded the cottage, but as we approached I realised it was a collection of life-sized carvings: a replica jungle of deer, eagles, wolves … It was an intriguing collection but, unimpressed by his own handiwork, Juna took us straight inside.

Inside the cottage, among sparse furniture, was cluttered with more works in progress; it appeared more like a workshop than a home. From one corner came a strange sound, scratching and rustling followed by a quiet 'coo'.

'What is that?' I asked.

'An owl,' Juna said, lifting Wanda down, sitting him on a chair.

Wanda's gaze was firmly fixed in the direction of the sound. He stood up and walked with shaky legs to a box in the corner. Inside, crouched in a nest of dry grass, a young bird looked out with beady eyes.

'*Hemaya, saylun, hansil,*' Wanda whispered to the bird, soothing words that the bird seemed to understand. He reached in, gently lifting out the owl, all the while whispering in the old tongue as he inspected the creature's injured leg, straightened by a small splint.

'He has a rare gift,' Juna said. 'I've heard there were people who could speak with animals, but I've never seen it before.'

'I've seen him with mice,' I said. 'It's the only time I've heard his voice. I don't think he's ever spoken to a person.'

Already the owl was tame to Wanda's hand. In a land of drought, I had considered his gift held no real significance other than to ease his loneliness; but here, in a wilderness where rain still fell, I wondered if his gift might hold some greater meaning.

'Where did you find the owl?' I asked.

'In the forest,' Juna said. 'Its leg was broken.'

I looked at him, hopeful; already I had seen more than I could have imagined.

'Is that the sacred forest?' I asked.

'The elders still call it that,' he said. 'It's where they live.'

The cottage was a self-sustaining small holding, complete with a well, roosting chickens, two goats, and a patch of ground cultivated with corn and root vegetables. The next morning, and the morning after, I helped with chores that began with milking the goats. In the afternoons I explored the surrounds, leaving Wanda recuperating in Juna's care.

Between Juna and me there was little conversation, an unspoken understanding to respect each other's personal space. I quietly wondered why he lived alone, separate from the community, but I never asked and he never offered an explanation. With Wanda, Juna was different. Juna chatted easily to my silent young friend, about the owl, and his many life-like sculptures; in turn, Wanda stayed close by his side. I thought often about their growing bond, considering it was borne from a mutual affinity and compassion for wildlife. While I was close to Wanda, and felt comfortable in the cottage, I felt like an outsider watching their friendship blossom. But each day, when I returned from exploring, I told Wanda of all I'd seen: purple heather, rabbits, and a strange creature covered in quills which Juna informed me was a porcupine. Wanda provided a captivated audience, always with the owl nestled in his lap. To see him carefree and content brought me joy, and in Juna's quiet home we both found a sense of peace.

But I couldn't forget the dusty streets and desert I had known as a child. Now more than ever I understood what my childhood home had lost. I thought of the elders and their mysterious spells, hanging onto life this side of the mountains, and wondered where I fit, where Mata fit. In the darkest place my mother had brought me a light; she was gifted with a message I had yet to understand. It was too long since I had looked into my crystal.

On the second night, with Juna in the hayloft upstairs, and Wanda asleep by the fire, I took out my crystal and held it in the palm of my hand. Just as before, the light appeared in its centre, glowing steadily brighter and revealing hues of blue and grey that swirled to become one. I dipped my fingers into the shroud of cool mist and slowly felt the physical world fall away. Standing in the mist, I saw my mother's face close by. I wanted to tell her of the valley and the creatures I had seen; I wanted to tell her that in a place where believers lived and rain still fell, surely here would lie answers to the Mantra's return. But in this place my words had no sound and she simply smiled, leading me on to a destination I was yet to find.

And so my nightly wanderings into the mist began again, oblivious to Wanda's watchful eyes.

Chapter 21

Wanda diligently cared for the owl, and in turn he was tended to by Juna, who ensured he rested and ate well. His strength was slowly improving, though the wound was still an open sore which Juna regularly cleaned and dressed with fresh poultice. By the morning of the fourth day, he was well enough to journey on to the forest riding on Juna's back. I watched him absorb the surrounds with wide eyes, eager and attentive as Juna shared his extensive knowledge of wildlife.

I tried to concentrate on Juna's words but my thoughts were distracted, increasingly so the further we ventured. I was excited to see the forest, but anxious as to how we would be received. Juna had said strangers weren't trusted; I could only hope I would be allowed to stay, after I told the elders about my mother.

Heading south west across the plains, up ahead the ground appeared to fall away. As we approached, a valley was slowly revealed, filled with a vast canopy of trees.

I stared in awe and said, 'I could never have imagined so many trees!'

'The forest used to spread all the way up this slope,' Juna said, leading the way down the embankment, 'but over time it died back. What's left still survives because of the people working it; they plant trees, feed wildlife, even spread a flower's seed. The elders say the rains used to last half a year or more; now we're lucky if they last a month.'

Still magical to my eyes, I said, 'But surely there's hope.'

'That's what the elders say. They pray for the Mantra's return, to restore the balance of nature. But I think the world's just becoming more imbalanced. Even in the forest, younger generations think the elders' beliefs are just superstition.'

Juna's cynicism was not entirely unexpected in light of the detached life he led, but it was the first time I had heard him allude to discord among the wider community. Despite his misgivings, for me, entering the forest was like stepping into another realm; the light, the air, the smells, combined to create a truly enchanting ambience. Green moss covered the ground like a blanket, vines wove patterns around trees, and curious sounds filled the air: leaves rustling, branches swaying, and chirping and warbling I could only imagine came from birds.

Further along the path, clouds of tiny flies swarmed around our heads. Wanda and I were soon scratching furiously, while Juna appeared immune and oblivious to our discomfort.

'We're being bitten,' I said.

Juna stopped, looked up at Wanda and then at me.

'I didn't think,' he said, veering off the path and searching the undergrowth. 'They never seem to bother me.' He returned with a bunch of swollen grass stems.

'Aloe grass,' I said, taking the stems and snapping some in half. Seeing Juna gently raise his eyebrows, I added, 'My mother knew herbal lore.'

I smeared sap on my face, handing a stem for Wanda to do the same. Slowly the irritation cooled.

There was so much to see, everything seemed to be moving: colourful butterflies, horned lizards, flying green beetles, stick insects... When we came across a troop of small brown monkeys looking down at us from the trees, I stopped and clasped my hands to my cheeks.

'Long-toed monkeys,' Juna said. 'The only monkey left. All other species have died out.'

'Why?'

'They relied on fruit,' he said, 'and when their food source died out, they starved.'

'So what do these monkeys eat?' I asked.

'Red ants.'

He pointed to the monkey closest to us. Looking at its foot gripping the tree, I saw one toe curiously long.

Juna said, 'It uses that toe like a hook, to dig ants out of nests in tree hollows.'

Juna's knowledge was infinite, from territorial turnbills, to the courtship display of hook-nosed bats. When finally he went quiet, I saw we were approaching a clearing; a village of round mud huts. It was a community bigger and more organised than I had expected. The air smelt strongly of bonfires and the sharp tang of soaking goat skins. Chickens roamed among gardens of sugar cane and beans; people were sat spinning thread, milking goats and tending crops.

A young girl was the first to see us, a stick of sugar cane hanging from her mouth. 'Ma!' she yelled, running to a woman sat milking a goat.

More faces looked up, suspicious. I took Juna's lead, lowering my eyes to avoid the glances, as we entered the village.

Juna led the way down narrow tracks, stopping outside one hut where he knocked on the door.

After a pause, a gruff voice from inside the hut said, 'Come in.'

Juna lifted Wanda down and opened the door, ducking down to step inside. I held Wanda's hand and followed into the darkened room. My eyes were soon stinging from the smoke of a small fire, and a pipe being passed around a circle of old men and women. Juna approached the elders, head bowed and hands clasped together. I stayed back with Wanda, keeping my eyes lowered, aware of the scrutinizing glances cast in my direction.

'Who are these people, Juna?' one old man said.

Hearing the sharp tone of his voice, I felt my cheeks grow hot.

'Sir,' Juna said. 'They arrived through the mist. The boy was sick, hit with a poison dart. The girl says the King is her enemy, that her mother was murdered for treason. They've no-where else to go.'

'Wah,' another man let out a breathy note of disapproval. 'How could they have got through the mist; a girl and a young boy?'

'You should have turned them away,' the first man said.

'They needed help,' Juna said. 'The boy almost died.'

'It's what the keepers are there for,' the man said. 'To stop spies getting through.'

'I mean no disrespect,' Juna said, keeping his head lowered, 'but I don't believe they're spies.'

'I must speak with the girl alone,' an old woman said; her words were met with stony silence.

I raised my eyes to find the speaker. An old woman met my gaze, with watery eyes that seemed filled with anticipation. She was the only elder wearing strings of beads around her neck and wrists, and wound around her hair, which was tied into a bun.

Juna took Wanda by the hand and made for the door; I met his eye, wishing he would stay, but he left with Wanda, closing the door behind them.

Nervous at being alone with the elders, I kept my eyes fixed on the woman wearing beads. She held my gaze as others spoke amongst themselves:

'There must be a weakness in the weave,' one man said. 'How else would they have got through?'

'They have to be spies,' said another. 'We've got no allies across the mountains.'

'Well, Juna wasn't a spy,' a woman said.

Juna? He doesn't come from here? It gave me hope that I might be able to stay.

'I said I need to speak with her alone,' said the woman wearing beads, speaking with quiet authority.

'Wise woman, but why?' the first man said. 'We have to decide as a council what to do with her.'

'Because I saw her arrival in the stones,' she said, brushing her hand across a curious collection of stones scattered on the ground beside her.

'Why haven't you said anything before?' he asked.

'Because my sight wasn't clear,' she said. 'I need to speak with her alone, to make sense of this.'

No more was said, and one by one the elders consented to the wise woman's wishes and left the hut.

Alone with the old woman, she clasped the beads around her neck and said, 'Blessed be the return of the Mantra. Blessed be the return of the rains.'

I smiled, warmed by the familiar prayer.

'What's your name, child?' she asked.

'Suni.'

'And your mother's name?'

'Mata.'

She took a deep breath, her eyes shining as she said, 'I'm known as Gogo now, but my birth name is Suni. You were named after me, child. I'm your great grandmother.'

Chapter 22

I stared at her in silent confusion. After years of struggle and pain, years of grief at the loss of my mother, it was hard to believe that all this time I had a great grandmother. I looked into her face, searching for the truth, stunned to see traces of Mata behind the sagging skin and deep wrinkles. She was a woman of legend, and she was alive. I felt the burden in my heart slowly ease. It was like coming home, finally.

Breathing in pipe smoke mixed with charred embers of the fire, I recalled aromas from the past: the musty pages of Mata's book; the earthy smell of fungus drying over coals; the smoky scent of Mata's hair. So much was familiar but we were strangers. I was eager to know her, eager to feel the closeness of kin.

'My mother told me about you,' I said, my voice trembling. 'She thought you had died.'

She didn't speak, just stared intensely into my eyes as she gently nodded.

'She showed me a picture you painted,' I said.

'A picture?'

'Of a mountain lion, from the days you took pilgrimage to the mountains.'

She glanced away, looking into the fire, as though the glowing embers revealed her distant past. I wanted to fill the silence with so many questions: I wanted to know what the world was like when she was a child; I longed to hear about pilgrimages and encounters with mountain lions and fighting with the resistance. I wanted her to put her arms around me, hold me close. But her sombre poise was something I recognised well, from my mother. She had seen decades come and go, maybe even a century; she had seen the world around her destroyed and changed. And now, here, at the centre of all things, she was the wise woman that even the elders looked to, with reserve in keeping with her status. Humbled by her presence, I rested my hands in my lap and patiently waited.

Her gaze drifted from the fire, resting on the scattered stones. To me they appeared inert, but her eyes flickered around as though reading something in them.

'What happened to your mother?' she finally said, looking back at me.

'She was a believer of the Mantra, accused of witchcraft. The King's men burned down my home with Mata inside.'

She reached across to rest her hand on mine, the soft, sagging skin of her fingers gently kneading mine. I kept my own hand still, savouring the feel of her touch until she rested her hand back in her lap.

'And was she gifted?' she asked.

'Yes,' I said. 'She was a seer. She saw the future in her dreams; my future. And after she died she found a way to come back to me.' I reached into the pocket of my smock and took out the crystal, holding it out for Gogo to see, anxious to think that finally I might find the answers to my mysterious gem. 'She led me to this.' I paused, looking at the crystal, anticipating the light, but it didn't come. 'I can't explain it, but sometimes when I look into the crystal I see a light, and mist. There's a whole world of mist inside, a place I can go; it's a place I see my mother.'

She glanced at the crystal only briefly, before gazing into my eyes as she said, 'You've come a long way, further than I can see. But I see you know the mists of *Serafay*.'

'*Serafay?*'

She said, 'Your mother was more than a seer. Dreamwalking is among the gifts handed down from mother to daughter. In my case it passed a generation, but not in yours. Aside from the dead, only a dreamwalker can know *Serafay*. It's a powerful gift, navigating *Serafay* to enter the dreams of others.'

Confused, I thought of the mist inside the crystal and said, 'My mother may have been gifted, but I only see what Mata shows me.'

'No, Suni,' she said. 'You see what you are meant to see, what you're open to see.' She raised the pipe to her lips and inhaled, blowing out a cloud of smoke. I gazed into the swirling patterns of grey, wondering at the depth of Gogo's gift. 'What about the boy you came with? He's not kin.'

'Wanda, no, but we're close like kin. *He's* gifted, to speak with animals.'

'He knows words of the old tongue?' she asked.

'Yes.'

'And you, do you know these words?'

'No,' I said.

She closed my hand around the crystal and said, 'The crystal is for you alone.'

'But my mother's trying to show me something,' I said. 'I think she has answers to the Mantra's return.' In the sacred forest, sitting with the wise woman, my great grandmother, it felt so tantalisingly close.

'Perhaps,' she said. 'But the stones are showing that the pattern to that great question is incomplete. The only thing my sight sees clearly is you, at the centre of all things.' Her mouth turned up into a gentle smile. 'I see you doubt yourself, Suni. But the time has come to step out of your mother's shadow, and realise that just as she was gifted, so are you. Like your mother you are a dreamwalker, and you come here bringing with you a gateway to *Serafay*, and a gifted boy. These things aren't coincidences; there are no coincidences.'

I lowered my eyes to look at the ground, wanting to hide my disbelief of the idea I was gifted as a dreamwalker. But I knew she saw what I tried to hide, just as I knew I would put my faith in my great grandmother; a believer of the Mantra. Mata had once said I had a part to play in the Mantra's return. I had seen so much that couldn't be ignored, but understood so little. The conviction in Gogo's voice, the sincerity on her face, brought strength after years of fear and uncertainty.

I raised my eyes to meet hers and asked, 'So what should I do?'

She leaned back, relaxing her shoulders, and said, 'You must have patience; we all must have patience. You are my great granddaughter, but in many ways we are strangers. Perhaps that's why the pattern is not clear to me, why *you* are not clear to me. You must find your place among us, start at the beginning, work in the forest and learn the old tongue.'

I was warmed by her welcome, but worried for Wanda.

'Wanda's still sick,' I said. 'He needs rest.'

Gogo said, 'The boy should stay close to Juna. His gift carries shades of light and dark.'

'What do you mean?' I asked, unsettled by the warning in her voice.

'The boy's gift is to speak with animals,' she said. 'I've only known one other person to possess that gift; Rhonad.'

'The King!' I said. 'How is that possible? The King's evil.'

She looked at me, one eyebrow raised, and said, 'You would condemn someone you've never known?'

'I don't understand,' I said. 'Wanda's a gentle child. I've seen him gain the trust of a timid mouse, and an injured wild animal. How could the King have the same gift when he slaughtered wildlife, even the mountain lions?'

'And yet even Rhonad was once just an innocent child,' she said.

Stunned to see the knowing look in her eyes, I asked in a whisper, 'You knew him?'

She nodded and said, 'I knew of him when we were both children; we were raised in neighbouring tribes. Like you said, Suni, only a gentle soul could bear the gift with animals, and in the beginning, Rhonad was gentle and timid and kind; back then I'd never have believed what would become of him as a man.' Her gaze drifted to look into the fire. 'But he was the only gifted child of his tribe, and so the elders favoured him. He grew up lonely, resented by the other children who I think were jealous of his favouritism. Loneliness was his downfall; it made him vulnerable to corruption. He must have been about twelve years old when he started speaking of Orag.'

'Orag?' I said. 'But Mata always said there's no such thing as an Earth Spirit.'

She looked back at me, eyes narrowed, and said, 'Orag is no Earth Spirit. It's a spirit of unnatural origins, but it's as real as you or I. It's true this land has only one creator, the Mantra, but like the roots of a tree the Mantra has an equal and opposite. For all the Mantra has the power to create, Orag has the power to destroy.'

I stared at her, wide-eyed.

Gogo said, 'It's told in the stories from ancient times; the creature of darkness arrived in the eye of a storm. The storm came in from the sea, with cloud so thick it obscured the sun. The whole land shook as great bolts of lightning struck the mountains with enough force to cut through rock. Summits crumbled, avalanches fell, and the creature of darkness flew down from the skies, disappearing into a crater on the western ridge. When the storm cleared, the mountains were reshaped, with the creature entombed inside. All these long years this ancient spirit has been trapped in its lair, sleeping.'

'But what is it?' I asked. 'Where did it come from?'

She said, 'For centuries our ancestors have told prophecies of its origin, its awakening, the chaos it will bring to our world. But for all the wisdom of our ancestors, all the threads told in the stones, there's little we know for certain. Rhonad is the only one who has heard it speak, an encounter that turned his sane mind to madness.' Gogo paused, then resumed, 'Like I said, his gift carries shades of light and dark. I've seen, in the stones, the day draw closer when we might all see it reveal itself. I see it longing to wake, to break free; I see its will grow, each day the miners dig. More than that, the thing I'm most certain of is that only the return of the Mantra can bring balance back to our land; without it, we're destined for a breaking of the world.'

The thought of Orag at the centre of all things, left me cold. I thought of the prayers of the miners and townspeople, all offering service to an ancient spirit trapped in the mountains, and Rhonad with his face hidden behind a shroud. *What monstrous face was he hiding?*

Chapter 23

I had believed my enemy was the King, just a man. If what Gogo said was true, there was a far more dangerous power that threatened us. I thought of the mountains, Orag's lair, with its crumbling tunnels. *They're digging too deep.* The thought left me cold. *Blessed be the return of the Mantra.*

'You're quiet,' Juna said, as we walked across the plains. 'What did Gogo say to you?'

I looked up at Wanda sitting on his shoulders. *Shades of light and dark.* I was tired of talking prophecies and doom.

'She said she's my great grandmother,' I said. I smiled to myself, liking the sound of the words.

Juna glanced at me, eyes gently narrowed, but said nothing.

'Why didn't you tell me you're also an outsider?' I asked.

I sensed his tension as he looked away, and felt awkward in the silence that followed. When a flock of birds flew overhead I was glad of the distraction.

'What are they?' I asked.

'Blue jays,' Juna said.

Blue jays, corn snakes and a wandering boar, kept the conversation light the rest of the way.

That evening, Wanda was asleep by the fire by the time dusk fell. I pulled the blanket in around him and kissed his forehead, happy to see him smile as he slept. For all Gogo's wisdom, I was sure she was wrong about him. His was a gift that the most timid creatures trusted.

Gifts and prophecies, I just wanted to relax. I went to the chest of drawers and hid the crystal at the back. Gogo said I was to learn; perhaps learning the old tongue would help me to see what Mata wanted to show me.

It was a while since I'd seen Juna. I opened the door and looked out, finding him sitting on a log leaning back against the cottage.

'Sorry about earlier,' I said, stepping outside. 'I didn't mean to pry.'

I stopped, smelling ale from the mug he was clutching in his lap; reminded of the brothel I considered going back inside.

'Come, sit with me,' he said, before taking a long sip as he looked out into the evening sky.

I hesitated, before pulling the shawl tight around my shoulders and sitting down next to him on the log: after everything he'd done for us, I couldn't offend him.

'Did Gogo tell you where I came from?' he asked.

'No.'

He turned to face me and said, 'I was born and raised at the palace.'

I sat back staring at him, sure I must have misheard. But the sombre look in his eyes, the grim line of his mouth, told me he was sincere.

'The palace?' I said. 'I don't understand.'

He looked down, staring into his mug and said, 'My father was a palace guard.'

I watched him raise the mug to his lips, slowly taking a long swig as he stared into space. Everything I knew about the palace guards, it seemed impossible that Juna's father was one of them. But then I remembered a time when I had thought the same about my own father. I thought back to the day Juna had found us in the mountains, how quickly he had gained Wanda's trust. I had had no choice but to trust him, a man I didn't know. But I had come to know him; he was a healer, with a deep compassion for the natural world; a man who had given us shelter; a man who the elders had granted permission to stay in the valley.

When he rested the mug back in his lap, I asked, 'How did you come to be here?'

'Same way as you,' he said. 'I escaped.' He glanced at me briefly before looking out into the evening sky. 'I hated my father like I hated all the guards; they were all the same, corrupt, cruel, violent... If it hadn't have been for my mother...' He paused, looking down at the mug. Moments of silence passed before he put the mug down on the ground. He rested his elbows on his knees, leaned forward with hands clenched tightly together.

I saw the sadness in his eyes, the tension in his jaw, and asked, 'What about your mother?'

He took a slow, deep breath and said, 'It was my mother who raised me; we lived together in the hut. All the women and children lived in huts among the goats and chickens. That's how we were treated. Actually, we were treated worse than the goats. Palace wives are slaves, beaten, forced to work from dawn 'til dusk in the gardens, or the kitchens. There was always plentiful food for the men, while the women and children survived on meagre rations. My mother always said she ate after I'd gone to bed, but she didn't. She went without so that I didn't go hungry.

'The men lived in the palace, eating, drinking, in the company of mistresses, just young girls. The wives were allowed no further than the kitchen, the children were told to stay out. But one night I snuck in. And after seeing the hallways, I never went back: the walls were covered in animal remains – skulls, tusks, antlers... Seeing that, I hated my father more. From infancy my mother had told me stories of a forest filled with wildlife, in a time when the rains fell, stories my father never knew she told me.'

Remembering similar memories I cherished from my own childhood, I said, 'You were close to your mother.'

He nodded and glanced down at the mug, hesitating before picking it up and taking another swig.

He said, 'I was fourteen when my father said he was sending me to the mines to work. I'd never heard my mother talk back to him before, but she did that night and she took a beating for it; I watched him beat her for days. I told her I'd go, but she wouldn't hear of it. She sat for nights sewing a ladder from old rags, and telling me about this valley, the only place my father would never find me. She talked about people living free by the old ways; I never thought to ask how she knew, never thought to ask much about her at all. She never spoke of life before me, of her family; I only knew she'd married young.' He turned to face me, eyes filled with regret. 'I pleaded with her to come with me, but she wouldn't. She told me not to look back and I didn't. I've got no idea what happened to her; I don't even know if she's still alive; I just left. I should never have left her.'

'You were just a child,' I said.

Seeing the shame on his face, I wanted to comfort him but could think of nothing to say. I'd come to the valley seeking safety, but was discovering truths I felt unprepared for: a creature of darkness threatening a breaking of the world, and Juna with the King's palace his origin... The world was more complex than I had imagined. So much suffering, so many people just trying to survive.

When he dropped his head to rest on my shoulder, I put an arm around him. A moment later he tilted his head to face me and brushed his lips against mine. The feel of his beard against my skin, his masculine aroma mixed with the smell of ale, I pulled back and stood up, threatened by his advance.

'I'm sorry,' Juna said. 'I didn't mean to do that.'

I shook my head and said, 'It's fine. It's just not what I'm looking for.'

'It's just the ale talking,' he said, standing up and making for the door. 'I need sleep. It won't happen again.'

When he closed the door behind him I sat back down, leaning forward to hug my knees. Gazing up at the starry sky I contemplated what my future might hold. Even before the brothel I'd never imagined my life with a man. But what did my life hold? I was in Gogo's hands, just as I had once been in Mata's. But was I destined for a life without romantic love? I didn't always want to be alone.

Chapter 24

I woke the next morning, tired and anxious after a restless night. I had seen Gusta's face in my dreams, smelt the stench of the brothel.

Juna set the table for breakfast, but he didn't join us. I sat with Wanda at the table, discreetly watching Juna busy sweeping the floor. He was an intuitive man and I feared he had sensed my vulnerability; I trusted him, but I didn't want him knowing about my life kept prisoner in the brothel. There was strain on his face as he focused on his work, avoiding looking in my direction. I wondered whether he regretted telling me of his past. Juna blamed himself for leaving his mother behind; perhaps taking in injured creatures was his way of searching for redemption.

Wanda finished his breakfast, got down from the table and went to the owl. Juna caught my eye; it was an awkward exchange and I was glad when he turned away and opened the door, brushing the sweepings out of the cottage.

With his back to me, Juna said, 'Wanda's tired after yesterday; I think he should stay here today. If you want to go to the forest, I'll stay here and look after him.'

I suspected it was just an excuse but I was glad of the offer; some time apart would do both Juna and I some good. I left Wanda content in looking after the owl, and set off for the forest alone.

I followed the same route as the day before; it was straight-forward to the embankment, but once in the forest I soon lost my way. Clambering through thick bush, I tried retracing my steps but feared I was becoming more lost. Seeing yellow eyes looking out from behind a bush, I stopped to watch two paws, a head, and the stealthy body of a big black cat step out of the undergrowth. Eyes fixed on me. I froze. The corners of its mouth curled back over fangs as it let out a long, low growl.

From behind, something came whooshing past my ear. I looked in surprise to see an arrow strike a tree just high of the cat's head.

'Yah, get out of here,' a woman yelled, running past me, shouting and waving her hands as she charged at the cat.

The cat leaned back on its haunches, hissing at the woman before slinking back, disappearing into the undergrowth.

I stared in astonishment at the fearless woman, as she retrieved her arrow from the tree and slipped it into the sling draped over her shoulder. When she looked at me and scowled, I lowered my eyes, intimidated.

'What are you doing out here?' she said.

She appeared a similar age to me, but the tone of her voice scolded. Based on her experienced handling of the bow and arrow, I suspected I was in the presence of a keeper.

'I got lost,' I said, feeling my cheeks grow hot.

The stern expression on her face slowly softened as she walked towards me.

'Are you Suni, Gogo's kin?'

I nodded.

Her lips turned up into a slow smile as she reached out to shake my hand.

'Khanyi's been waiting for you,' she said. 'I'm Zandi. Come, I'll take you to the village.'

I looked back into the bushes and asked, 'What was that?'

She put a hand on my shoulder, guiding me back to the path, and said, 'A black leopard. They don't usually attack; she must have cubs. It's better to charge than show fear.'

From the moment I met Zandi I was curious about her; her appearance was different to other women I'd known. She was dressed in shorts and a vest pulled tight, flattening her small breasts; her hair was styled away from her face, in rows of plaits clinging to her scalp.

In the mines I had sought to appear as a boy but this woman claimed androgyny as her own, as she walked with a swagger.

Walking together through the forest she said, 'I've wondered about you. No-one's ever got past me in the mist before; one moment you were there, the next you were gone.'

I slowed my steps and said, '*You* shot Wanda?'

'I'm a keeper,' she said, unfazed. 'You're lucky it was me: not many of us use darts now. How is the boy?'

'Recovering,' I said. 'Juna's looking after him.'

She looked at me, frowning, and said, 'You should watch out for Juna; he's not one of us. Did you know he came from the palace?'

'He told me,' I said, glad to have been forewarned.

'It doesn't seem to worry the elders, but if you ask me, you can't be sure what side he's on.'

I was in no doubt over Juna's loyalty to the valley, but I didn't want to start a disagreement with a keeper I barely knew.

She paused to pull a stalk of grass, chewing on the succulent stem as she said, 'At least there's no doubt about you, Gogo's great granddaughter; you've got the whole village talking. Keepers returned from the mist this morning, claiming to have sighted a mountain lion up there. Mountain lions haven't been seen for years. Villagers are claiming it's down to you; they say you're going to bring back the Mantra.'

The speculation made me uncomfortable.

When I didn't respond, she said, 'You'll have to get used to it, being kin of the wise woman. Here people live by Gogo's prophecies and premonitions seen in the stones and stars. And everything, all the elders' hopes for the future, are based on the Mantra returning: a spirit that no one alive has ever seen.'

'You don't believe in the Mantra?' I asked.

'I believe what I see,' she said. 'The enemy is at our borders and the keepers protect the borders. We have to save ourselves.'

She stopped where the path branched, pointing down the track veering right.

'It's straight down that path,' she said. 'You'll see the village.'

I watched her head off in the opposite direction, my gaze lingering until she disappeared. Meeting this straight talking woman had been refreshing.

Approaching the village I was greeted by a strange melody of drumming and chanting. I felt moved by the harmony, swayed by the perfectly pitched notes that filled the air as I made my way through the narrow lanes, watched by the villagers. Nearing Gogo's hut, the harmony grew louder and the words clearer; words of the old tongue sung by the elders gathered inside. The door was closed and I stopped, not knowing whether I was supposed to interrupt.

I heard a voice call my name. I turned to see a woman, waving as she approached.

'Gogo asked me to meet you,' she said, shaking my hand. 'I'm Khanyi.'

'What's happening in there?' I asked, glancing back at the door.

'The elders are weaving the mist-binding spell,' Khanyi said. 'You're to come with me, to learn the ways of the forest. Learning the old tongue will bring you closer to the Mantra.' She wrapped both her hands around mine and said, 'It's an honour to meet you. Everybody here wants to meet you. You bring us all hope of the Mantra's return.'

Locked in her gaze, my hands clasped in hers, I gritted my teeth and forced a smile for this woman who appeared old enough to be my mother.

In the days that followed, assigned by Gogo, Khanyi was my mentor. She was a kind, intelligent woman, with a seemingly infinite knowledge of the forest. In many ways she reminded me of my mother, with her dedication to the practise of herbal lore, and unwavering belief of the Mantra. Each morning I met her in the forest, where she taught me to identify plants, trees and animals, complete with their names in the old tongue. It was a language difficult to pronounce, but Khanyi patiently taught me to roll my tongue as I attempted the breathy notes and clicks.

I met many people on our walks, all tirelessly working: planting trees, feeding wildlife, and pollinating flowers. I was amazed by the intricacy of the work, in particular the dedication given to pollination. Pollinating morning flowers, *mharix shlaa,* involved collecting Ngava beetles, *Nghaa,* and individually placing them in the opened flowers early evening. Overnight, the petals closed, trapping the beetle inside while the flower produced a dusting of yellow seeds. In the morning, when the petals opened, the dust-covered beetles flew off to pollinate the next flower. In particular I enjoyed the children's version, of tying string to a beetle's leg, and flying it like a kite. It was a game frowned on by adults, who punished with stories of an evil King who steals naughty children in their sleep.

The afternoons were spent with Gogo. It was a time of silent meditation, to 'look inwards and reflect'. She told me the importance of patience and the need to be still, since only then would I be able to truly listen. These were my hardest lessons, since all I heard were memories I had worked hard to forget. In silence there was no distraction and no escape. Nightmares of the brothel plagued my sleep, leaving me tired by day. Still I persisted, hoping each night when I looked into my crystal something more would be revealed. But always it was the same, Mata leading me on seemingly to no-where.

Two weeks passed and I was growing restless. I remained obedient to Gogo's will, but I was doubting the methods more and more. And I was doubting myself. Plagued by grim and painful memories, I was forced to look at the path behind me, at all the events that had led me to where I was now. Alone in the mines I had been just a girl, afraid, missing my mother. I had thought the crystal to be enchanted, a gift that would reveal to me how to bring about the Mantra's return. But what if it was nothing more than my mother coming back to offer me comfort? What if Mata's vision had been nothing more than her own yearning for life to return to the land? It was a time of confusion, learning, reciting, and being still. And yet I knew that while people were living freely in the forest, others, innocent people, were still suffering in the mines, the brothel and the town. All the King had created, all the suffering to the land, the animals, and the people, this was why the Mantra had left; this was what the Mantra had condemned. Reciting words from the natural world just wasn't enough.

Chapter 25

One afternoon, leaving the Gogo's hut after meditation, I crossed Zandi in the lanes. She stopped and asked, 'How's it going with Khanyi?'

I nodded and said, 'She knows a lot about the forest.'

'I've seen you with her,' she said. 'You have the same look on your face I used to have.'

'What do you mean?' I asked.

'I mean you don't look like you believe in it,' she said.

I glanced around, glad to see no one close enough to overhear.

'Gogo says learning about the forest, learning the old tongue, is my path,' I said.

'And?' she said, one eyebrow raised. 'Have you had any revelations?'

I folded my arms and said, 'You're making fun of me.'

She reached out to touch my arm and said, 'I don't mean to. I'm just asking.'

'And I'm just learning,' I said. 'Gogo tells me to be patient.'

'Well, that's one way,' she said.

'And what would you suggest I do?'

'Join us; join the keepers.'

'You're not serious!'

'Why not?' she asked.

'Well for one thing, I've never fired an arrow in my life.'

'There's more to being a keeper than firing arrows,' she said. 'Besides, I'm a good teacher.' She squeezed my arm. 'I am serious. We could really use you. Don't you think protecting the valley from invasion is more useful than learning names of plants, or sitting in the dark meditating?'

She was putting my own thoughts into words. It was the only thing that made sense, fighting the enemy to preserve what the Mantra stood for.

But first I had to speak with Gogo.

'Are you sure this is your path?' Gogo asked, after I'd finished explaining.

I had expected her to refuse, not take my request seriously.

Seeing she was willing to listen, I said, 'I think it's the right thing for me. I've learnt so much and I know you say to be patient. I know the answers are there, and I want to find them; I just think there's another way.'

She looked at me, eyes searching. 'You have my blood. Your path should be clear to me, but it's not. The keepers are non-believers. They can't lead you to the Mantra, and yet I see your desire and all of our destiny go hand in hand.' She brushed a hand over the stones. 'There's so much of you I still can't see, so many threads I don't have answers for. But you've been chosen for this quest, and we must have faith in you.'

The rest of the elders were not so harmonious, demanding patience and insisting that living in accordance with the old ways was the way forward. But the world had changed; I had changed. Gogo had said it herself; the time had come to walk out of Mata's shadow, and the way of the elders had been Mata's way.

Zandi was there to meet me as I left the hut.

'How did it go?' she asked.

'I'm joining the keepers,' I said, feeling suddenly nervous at the prospect.

She smiled and said, 'Don't worry, you're one of us now. We'll start training in the morning.'

Up to now I had seen Zandi as a strong, bold woman, steadfast in her convictions, but as she accompanied me back through the forest, I saw a softer side.

'I've never left this valley,' she said, idly sweeping her hand through long grass as we walked. 'I've never seen further than the mountains. What's it really like where you come from?'

'It's just desert,' I said. 'I've never seen rain. Nothing grows, there's no wildlife. My mother used to tell me stories about forests, and about the Mantra. She always said it would never rain again unless the Mantra returned.'

'You were close to your mother?' Zandi said.

'She was all I had.'

'What was she like?' she asked.

In Zandi's company the words flowed easily, as I recalled life before the fire. She probed for details, until I imagined the feel of Mata brushing my hair, and the taste of tea sugared just how she liked it. Where I had felt confusion, Zandi saw simple truths, clarity that felt reassuring. I kept to a slow pace, wanting to draw out the time. When we reached the edge of the forest, she hugged me goodbye. I felt my stomach strangely flutter and knew I was anxious to see her again.

Stepping out from beneath the forest canopy, I saw the sky filled with dark grey clouds. The air was thick with humidity, and by the time I reached the top of the embankment my whole body was doused in sweat. The first drop of rain hitting my forehead came as a surprise. It pooled in my eye as I looked up at the clouds in eager anticipation. After a long pause, a sudden downpour of rain came cascading with such force, it created a din that sounded like drums. Drenched, hair sticking to my face, clothes clinging to my skin, I held my arms up to the sky.

By the time I reached Juna's cottage, I had mud up to my knees. Wanda was standing in the doorway, one hand held out to feel the rain.

'It's raining,' he said, as I approached.

I stared at him, stunned to finally hear him speak, and crouched down next to him in the doorway.

'What did you say?'

'It's raining,' he said again.

I looked up at Juna standing behind him, saw him nod and smile at me.

'He was just ready,' Juna said.

I looked back at Wanda, watched his face break into a smile, and held his face in my hands as I kissed his forehead.

'It's so wonderful to hear you speak,' I said.

'Come inside,' Juna said. 'You need to get dry.'

I went to the fireplace, while Wanda fetched the owl.

'Look, Suni,' Wanda said, as he put the owl down on the ground and stepped back.

There was no longer a splint on the owl's leg, and when Wanda beckoned the bird to him, it hopped and flapped its wings all the way to Wanda. I smiled to see the pride on Wanda's face, and to hear the owl chirp; even to my amateur ears it sounded to have more cheer in its coo.

Over a mug of tea, Wanda and Juna told me their plans to release the owl back into the forest, and their hopes that one day it might have chicks of its own.

'And Juna's teaching me to carve,' Wanda said.

He fetched a lump of wood to show me. Looking among the lumps and hollows, I was at a loss.

'The shape of the owl's eyes are coming on,' Juna said.

I spotted two odd-shaped hollows, and ran my fingers over them.

'Yes, I see,' I said.

We chatted long into the evening. It was such a joy to listen to Wanda, to know that finally he felt safe and confident enough to let down his barrier. I watched him long after he fell asleep, thinking over all the stages of his young life. Circumstance had brought us together, and in each other we had both found someone we could trust. There were few people in my life I'd known as well as Wanda. Even with my mother there had been so many secrets. There was a time I'd felt close to Ntombi, but the brothel, and Wiseman, had pushed us apart. I trusted Juna, but it was a trust that could only go so far. My last thought was of Zandi. We had only just met but already I felt close to her.

Chapter 26

The next morning I arrived in the forest, invigorated by the vivid colours and smells of a landscape soaked in rain. The forest canopy gave shelter, aside from intermittent showers as leaves gave way under the weight of pooling water.

Zandi was waiting for me. She reached up, brushing aside a lock of wet hair hanging over my face. It was a touch that lingered, strong and delicate in the same breath, leaving me with a curious warm feeling inside. As she led the way I found myself watching the subtle beauty captured in her self-assured poise; strong and elegant.

She took me on an unfamiliar path, to a place where elderbirch grew, and sat beneath a big old tree with long sturdy boughs radiating outwards.

'Come, sit with me,' she said, patting the dry moss next to her.

'I thought we were training?' I asked.

'We are,' she said. 'But like I said, it's not just about firing arrows.'

I sat beside her, curious.

She said, 'I wanted to ask about when you crossed the mist. I only shot the dart because you managed to get so close; no one gets close to a keeper. I only sensed you for a moment and after I'd shot the dart, I lost sense of both of you. I can't figure out how you got past us. It's never happened before.'

I shrugged my shoulders and said, 'What about Juna? He crossed the mountains.'

'Far east of here, where we don't patrol,' she said. 'The King's men only attempt the path from the mines; the path you came on.'

I thought of the blinding mist with its haunting voices, apparently a spell of the elders to ensnare the enemy. Looking back I realised how lucky we had been to make it through, and how lucky Wanda was to have survived. Zandi had been there, had seen us clear enough to hit Wanda with a dart.

'How do you do it?' I asked. 'How do you see anything in the mist?'

I had thought Zandi to be a pragmatic person, believing in only earthly things, and I had expected the keepers to follow a simple path in comparison to the mysteries of the elders' teachings. But I was wrong. Zandi spoke of things I'd never heard of before: the Abyss, the origin of all things, also known as the Great Cradle, an eternal void of pure darkness absent of all else, even time. She spoke of the origin of life itself: a spark of light, the first light, shone out from the Abyss, creating the life force that brought into being all forms of life; the First Dawn.

'Life force?' I said, struggling to follow her reasoning. 'I didn't think you believed in a spirit.'

'I don't,' she said. 'I'm not talking legend. The elders would tell you the Mantra created the Abyss; it doesn't matter either way. The Abyss brought the first light, and that light still echoes today. These echoes are strands of energy you can connect to; they connect all things. The elders manipulate these strands, weaving them to create mist in the mountains; the keepers harness this energy to unlock a hidden sense, a sense that guides us through the mist.'

It was hard to imagine, hard to follow, and yet she appeared completely sincere.

'I'll show you,' she said. 'Come, stand up.'

She untied the sash from around her waist, placed it over my eyes, and tied it tight at the back of my head.

'What are you doing?' I said, feeling her adjust it over my eyes. 'I can't see anything.'

'That's the point,' she said. 'You won't find your hidden sense with your eyes open; sight's only a distraction. I want you to look into the dark and focus your mind. Think of nothing but the void. When your mind's clear, and all you know is the void, then you'll be open to the echoes of light. Focus on a spark, think only of that light, feel the warmth of its glow, give yourself to it, let it unlock your hidden sense.'

Standing blindfolded in the forest, hearing Zandi's instructions that seemed so unlike her, at first I wondered whether she was playing a prank. She didn't speak again, but I could hear her breathing. The depth of what she'd told me had taken me by surprise, and I wasn't sure if I really believed it. But it was the first time I'd ever been given a real explanation. I had spent days with Gogo, but always in silent meditation. This at least felt tangible, more so than learning words of the old tongue to somehow forge a mysterious connection with a Great Spirit. The idea of a light in the dark made me think of the light in the crystal. It had just appeared, seemingly from nowhere, a light that had guided me. And so I tried looking into the darkness, concentrated on ridding my mind of all thoughts. I focused and I waited, but there was nothing.

'I can't see anything,' I said.

'That's because you think the Abyss is darkness, and you see darkness as fear. But the Abyss is pure void. The only way to see it is to detach yourself from your feelings; clear all thoughts from your mind. You'll only see the lights when you're looking into pure void.'

I took a deep breath and focused. Thoughts intruded the quiet, but one by one I pushed them aside. I was left longing to see the lights, and this I also pushed aside. As the sounds of the forest faded into the distance, I felt a cold sense of calm that tempered the warmth of the day. A faint light flickered. I was immediately struck by the feeling of triumph and the light disappeared. I refocused and saw the light reappear, first one spark and then more.

I pushed up the blindfold and said, 'I saw it; I saw sparks of light.'

Zandi looked mildly surprised.

'I knew there was something about you,' she said. 'For most people it takes weeks to see anything. You must have felt the Abyss before, maybe when your mother was killed.'

I thought back to the day Mata died, the day my world collapsed. I had felt so cold and detached; I thought I might die too. It was a cold feeling that had grown familiar: I felt it each time I entered the mist of the crystal; remembered it from the dream I had had whilst crossing the mountains, of Mata at market; it was the same cold I had felt seeing Mata's apparition in the mines. All my doubt and confusion faded. In the darkest place Mata had shown me a light born from the Abyss. Now I was training to be a keeper, protectors of the valley guided by the same lights. I could not believe as the elders did, that the keepers had no place on the path to the Mantra's return. My belief in the quest was restored.

Zandi was watching me closely.

'Try again,' she said. 'But this time try holding onto the sparks.'

I pulled the blindfold back down and focused on the Abyss. One by one, sparks of light appeared in the dark. I focused, tried to imagine them drawing closer, but the lights faded returning to dark. I tried again and again, each time seeing the lights, and each time they faded.

'I see them,' I said. 'But I can't hold onto them.'

'You're clearing your mind, but not far enough,' Zandi said. 'You have to face the void, let everything go.'

In several more attempts, I made no progress. The effort of concentrating finally left me feeling drained.

'I can't do it,' I said, taking the blindfold off.

Zandi tilted my chin to face her. I was afraid she would see what I wanted no one to see.

'What are you holding onto?' she said. 'What happened to you?' I wanted to look away but her gaze left me compelled. 'Tell me.'

Once I started I couldn't stop. Words came spilling out as I told of every encounter I'd had in the brothel, from Khalid who violently stole my youth, to Gusta and all the others who had left me battered and used. And finally, when I realised my father was no better, a disappointment that had broken my heart. I had carried shame and anger, but the more I spoke the lighter I felt. Zandi never said a word, nor altered her patient, unassuming expression. When finally I stopped, she put her arms around me and hugged me tightly to her chest. I felt the softness of her skin against my cheek and thought how I didn't want her to let go. Finally she relaxed her arms, releasing me from the embrace. Standing face to face, our eyes locked, I tilted my head towards her, brushing my lips against hers. She kissed me back; a long lingering kiss.

When she pulled back, she held my face in her hands and said, 'You've got more reason to fight than any of us. Use it. When the time comes, show no mercy.'

I felt different inside, stronger. Looking into the void, one light was shining brighter than the rest. I held it in my sights, felt a tingling sensation on my tongue. As the light grew brighter, the tingling moved to my lips and the whole of my face. It rushed down my limbs to the tips of my fingers and toes, a feeling so intense it made my heart race and head spin. A surge of nausea forced me to bend forward. I ripped off the blindfold, struggling to get my breath.

Zandi said, 'That was your hidden sense. Don't resist it; you need to accept it. It's stronger than all your other senses. Once you've embraced it, you'll sense everything around you like a map in your mind's eye.'

I looked again, feeling my entire body tingling and heart racing. Nausea subsided as I pushed forward, leaving the pit of my stomach cold. Only my feet touched ground, but my fingers felt wet moss and gritty earth. Awareness of my surroundings grew until it was all consuming; the feel of rough bark, blades of grass, leaves glistening with dew. At first it felt overwhelming, and random, but slowly I felt the order. I took a step forward and to the side, sensing the rock. Between two bushes, I arrived at a tree. I took the blindfold off and looked back, seeing the path I had safely navigated.

'Put the blindfold back on,' Zandi said.

She had moved to the side, her own eyes covered. I pulled the blindfold back down. The sparks of light came, along with the rushing sensation that brought to life my hidden sense.

'Now look at me,' she said, her voice was sounding with an echo.

I turned to face her, seeing shapes created from the sparks of light, coloured with shades of blue and pale yellow. A bird flew past, its body orange and the tips of its wings blue like stone. Zandi was there, the centre of her core glowing deep red that faded to orange and then yellow at the reach of her limbs.

Seeing her walk towards me, I took off the blindfold and said, 'I saw you.'

She was watching me, curious.

'And I saw you,' she said. 'I've never seen a weave like yours before.'

'What do you mean?'

'When you looked at me, what did you see?' she asked.

'Colours; red and orange.'

She said, 'Our hidden sense sees hot and cold; red shows the warmth of the body, blue shows the cold of a stone. But you, you were pale yellow.'

Chapter 27

I soon mastered the art of looking into the Abyss, harnessing the light and navigating blindfolded. Zandi thought I had natural talent, but I thought it was down to years of practise looking into my crystal. But I never mentioned the crystal to Zandi. My training as a keeper needed to be *my* journey, the first decision I had made for myself that didn't involve fleeing danger.

The day came when I was ready to move on to the bow and arrow.

The bow was heavier than I thought, and the effort of keeping the bowstring taut while focusing my aim soon left my arms and shoulders aching. The first arrow I fired dropped to the ground barely an arm's length away; the second and third arrows didn't travel much further. But Zandi was a patient teacher, helping me to guide my aim onto the target she had marked out on a tree, and by noon the arrows were closing in.

Taking a break in the shade of an elderbirch, picnicking on flatbreads, two women arrived. By the bows and arrows across their backs they were obviously keepers, but it was what they dragged behind them that caught my attention: a stuffed sack, crudely sewn to resemble a body, head, and bulging limbs.

'We thought it was about time we met the new recruit,' one woman said, reaching down to shake my hand. 'I'm Nita; this is my sister, Bindi.'

'You've been keeping her to yourself,' Bindi said to Zandi, a sly smile on her face. She turned to me and said, 'You should watch out for Zandi; she's known for breaking hearts.'

'Take no notice,' Zandi said to me. 'She's just stirring.'

Bindi looked at me, smiled and said, 'She's right, I'm just teasing.'

Nita dropped the stuffed sack in front of us and said to me, 'We thought you could use this. Don't tell Gogo, but we call it Rhonad. Hitting a tree's one thing, but it's not the same as killing a man; sink your arrow into the dummy and you'll start to get the idea.'

I looked at the head with stitching resembling eyes, a nose and a mouth.

'Are you off?' Zandi said, as the sisters turned to leave.

Bindi looked back and said, 'Wouldn't want to interrupt your cosy lunch.' She looked at me and added, 'Remember what I said about her, fickle in love, that's Zandi.'

I watched them leave then turned to Zandi, one eyebrow raised.

'What did she mean by that?' I asked.

'She thinks of herself as my ex,' Zandi said. 'It was a long time ago and I would hardly call it an affair. She'd deny it, but she was never into girls. She's with Yuba now and has been for a long time. He's one of the keepers.'

She reached across to stroke my hair and I leaned in to kiss her.

When I pulled away she said, 'I think I'm the one in danger of getting my heart broken.'

I smiled and shook my head. 'You've got nothing to worry about with me.'

She stood up and reached for my hand, pulling me to my feet.

'Come on,' she said. 'Let's sink some arrows into Rhonad.'

She positioned the dummy at the edge of the clearing, leaning it against a stick to keep it in an upright position. I nocked an arrow and went to take aim, but hesitated.

'I've never killed a man,' I said. 'I've never killed anything bigger than a fish.'

Zandi came to stand behind me, reached round to hold my arms in position as I took aim.

She whispered in my ear, 'Think of the faces who killed your mother; think of the men who hurt you in the brothel. This is your time to fight back.'

I steeled my composure, jaw clenched, eyes staring at the target, as I released arrow after arrow into the dummy's heart. It was for more than revenge, it was for the valley, the forest, for life itself.

I watched an arrow land dead centre, thinking of Wiseman's face and every bruise Ntombi had sustained.

'I'll go back to the brothel, one day,' I said, walking towards the dummy to retrieve the arrows.

'What are you talking about?' Zandi asked.

'Wanda's aunt, my friend, Ntombi, I left her behind,' I said. 'Will you come back with me some day? Will you help me get her out?'

'It's not possible,' she said, walking towards me. Standing face to face, she held onto my arms.

'But I know a way in,' I said. 'The same way I got out. I can't bear to think of her down there, kept like some sort of slave, married to a man that beats and humiliates her.' I held up the bow. 'I left her behind, but I've got this now.'

'There's no going back, Suni,' she said. 'We don't go further than the mist. The King's men far outnumber us, but in the mist they're like flies caught in a spider's web. The enemy fear us because they know nothing about us; their fear keeps the valley safe, as much as the mist or the keepers do. If we show ourselves to them, we lose that fear. If they wanted to they could cross east along the ridge, where Juna came. We haven't the numbers to patrol there, but they don't know that. They don't know anything about us, and we have to keep it that way. Just imagine what they'd do to this valley if they got through.'

Days turned into one week, then two. I was training alongside the other keepers, firing mock arrows as I practised my aim, blindfolded, on moving targets. They were a tight-knit group, but I had advanced quickly and they welcomed me; though my cool form in view of their other sense was a source of confusion. My own hidden sense revealed the world around me with crisp clarity; like a game of cat and mouse, practising my aim on glowing bodies that tried to evade me.

Finally the day came when I was ready to join a tour of the mist.

Riding bareback on a herd of wild horses, ten keepers galloped across the plains, heading for the mountains. Having only ever ridden a mule, I clung to Zandi, cheeks burning as wind and rain whipped against my face. Nearing the mountains I looked across the range of summits, eyes fixed on the two peaks that had been my point of crossing. I was in the company of warriors, but faced with the mountains our numbers felt too few. The mines were swarming with the enemy, an enemy that had enslaved me. I thought of Gogo fighting alongside the resistance, face to face with the enemy, and Mata, facing danger with courage as she upheld the truth; they were my kin, and now we had the mist. Having tasted freedom I gritted my teeth, ready for the chance to defend it.

High in the foothills we rode out of the rain, and left the horses behind to graze. Trekking up the rocky pass, I kept my eyes on the ground. According to Gogo we were tramping over Orag's lair, an ancient spirit trapped beneath rock and stone. I could only wonder what chaos would be unleashed if it woke.

We arrived at the keepers' camp nestled in the shade of a rocky tor, where men and women sat lounged around a bonfire. I hadn't expected to find them appear so relaxed, but their week-long patrol had been uneventful. Our own party divided into two groups, and while one group remained at camp, I set off with Zandi and the rest of my group, climbing the pass to complete the first watch.

High in the mountains we rounded a crag and were met by tendrils of mist.

Zandi reached out to touch my arm and said, 'Are you ready?'

'Yes.'

'Stay alert,' she said. 'We can go weeks, months, without encountering the enemy, but they still come, and they're armed.'

'I'm ready,' I said, eyes fixed on hers, determined not to let my comrades down.

She smiled and said, 'I know you are. You've been in the mist before; you know what to expect. Just don't let the voices of the dead distract you.'

'I won't.'

I armed my bow and stepped forward, feeling the cool haze sweep over my face. Hearing the sound of distant voices, I felt comforted by the thought that among them, the elders were speaking. I closed my eyes, silenced all thought, and focused on the void. Sparks of light shone from the abyss, and the familiar cold came rushing through me, bringing to life my hidden sense. I saw the heat of my companions, and the cool contours of the rough terrain, and joined the hunt.

Time lost meaning: born from the void, the lights were eternal, an energy that kept us alert as we moved as a group, evenly spaced, like a fishing net dragged through water. We patrolled the area in laps, until the route was so familiar I could anticipate the obstacles around each corner. Still I moved my bow arm from side to side, scanning the area, alert to the unexpected.

There came a sound from behind, heavy breathing and clumsy feet scuffing on the ground. I swung round. Yuba had been behind me, but I knew it wasn't Yuba I could sense nearby: the glowing figure was stumbling, blind, holding out a long sharp dagger of cool blue, stabbing the air in random strikes. I aimed my arrow centre of his core, my bow arm pulled taut. He came closer, but still I didn't release the arrow. To my horror, my hidden sense was fading, replaced by fear and confusion. *Does he deserve to die?*

I was looking out blind, heard a heavy thud followed by the clang of metal on stone.

A moment later a hand rested on my shoulder and Yuba whispered, 'If you're not ready, go back. There could be more out here. If you can't do what's necessary, you'll be a liability.'

He let go of my shoulder and moved away. Fear turned to shame at my failure; Yuba had probably just saved my life. *Mata didn't deserve to die. The keepers don't deserve to die.* I pulled back an arrow and held the bow out, arms taut, determined not to fail again.

I closed my eyes and let my thoughts drift until there was only the void. At one with the mist I moved silent over the mountainous terrain, focused on the shades of cool blue that shaped the path, and the glow of my comrades with stealthy, purposeful movements. Everything belonged. Until, up ahead, a figure glowing deep red stumbled awkwardly down a steep section of path. I focused my aim, released the arrow, and watched it hit dead centre.

The moon was full when I followed Zandi clear of the mist. The next group were there to replace us, all eyes on Yuba and Chad as they dragged two bodies out of the mist. I was shocked to see how young one of the men looked; he couldn't have been more than eighteen years old. I was a keeper, protector of the valley, and I had killed a man little older than a boy. Zandi put a hand on my shoulder and squeezed.

'You did good,' she said with a smile.

I hesitated before smiling back. Khalid hadn't been much older, but he had been old enough to rape me.

The bodies were dragged down the pass, across the levelled ground of camp, and half dragged, half carried up the rocky tor.

'The wolves will finish them off,' Zandi said, as they were pushed unceremoniously over the edge and down the mountainside.

My mouth set in a grim line as I considered what would happen on the lower slopes when the wolves arrived. I thought back to my own arrival, and how close Wanda and I had been to such a grisly fate.

Huddled beneath a blanket with Zandi, I tried focusing on the rise and fall of her chest as she fell asleep easily. In just a few hours our next shift would start, but while I was tired, my mind wouldn't rest, unsettled by the distant sound of wolves howling. I shifted onto my side, nestled my face into the nape of her neck and listened to the rhythm of her breaths. My thoughts turned to Wanda, a gifted boy who had found refuge in the valley, a place of safety where he was finally able to speak. It was my last thought as I finally drifted to sleep.

The mist was all around me with ghostly faces drifting by. The air was cool and still and silent, like the mist in the crystal. I looked among the passing faces for Mata, but couldn't see her. I walked forwards, searching for my mother, and felt a change in the air: a gentle breeze brushed against my face, and a soft rushing sound I couldn't distinguish. The further I went the breeze grew stronger and the sound louder, like the ebb and flow of a tide, or wind brushing through leaves. Looking into the blinding haze I realised the ghostly faces were gone, but something else caught my eye. There was a subtle change in the silvery grey haze, a patch of darker colouring that became more distinguishable in its differing tones of grey as I walked towards it, my hair blowing back in the breeze. As I closed in upon it I saw it was a place where the mist parted, like a window into another world: it was a world of forest, dark and eerie as though it was dead; a place where nothing stirred except the breeze blowing through bare branches. I thought to turn back, confused by where the mist had led me, afraid of the unfamiliar world. But a flash of colour caught my eye. I strained to see but it disappeared behind the trees. A moment later it reappeared, a person, a child, the only sign of life, moving through the lifeless forest. When the child stopped and turned to look in my direction, I saw it was Wanda.

In the mist I had no power to speak; still I tried calling his name, but the sound of my voice died away before the words had left my lips. I saw him, but he appeared not to see me as he roamed the area as though exploring. Every so often he stopped to look among the decayed foliage, as though fascinated. I wondered whether he could see things hidden from me, and, as the moments passed, I realised that the colour of his skin and his clothes were fading to grey, at one with the surrounds. Desperate to reach him I rushed forwards, but no matter how many steps I took, the gateway was in front and I was still in the mist. He was walking away from me, deeper into the trees. Creeping vines were slowly moving up and out from the tree trunks, reaching out to close the gap behind Wanda, until I lost sight of him. I was running, but the forest remained out of reach.

'Suni, wake up.' I opened my eyes to see Zandi leaning over me. She brushed the hair from my sweat-drenched brow and said, 'You were having a nightmare.'

I stared into her eyes, feeling a tear spill down the side of my face and my chest tight with the urge to cry. The sense of loss was confusing, until the dream came back to me; I knew it was no ordinary dream.

I sat up and said, 'I have to get to Wanda; something's wrong.'

She put a hand on my shoulder and said, 'It was just a dream.'

'No,' I said, wiping the tear from my eye. It had felt so real, still did. Dreams were born from memory, but I had no memory of a dead forest. I pushed the blanket aside and stood up.

'Suni, it's the middle of the night,' Zandi said. 'At least wait until morning.'

'Please, Zandi,' I said. 'I have to go; I need your help.'

Chapter 28

Riding with Zandi over the plains, I watched dawn tease the night sky with wispy plumes of red and orange. I found myself looking into the complex patterns, wondering if a seer would read prophecies told in the sweeping designs. It was the start of a new day, and I feared what this day would bring.

Arriving at Juna's cottage, I jumped down from the horse and ran inside. I stopped to see Wanda laid out by the fire with Juna watching over him. Juna turned to face me; one look at his tear-stained face and I feared the worst.

'He's gone,' Juna said, his voice cracking. 'I don't understand why. I thought he was getting better.'

I held a hand to my mouth and walked towards them, collapsing to my knees beside Wanda. I touched his hair, stared down at his face, willing his eyes to open, but they didn't. Juna buried his face in his hands as I scooped Wanda into my arms, resting him against my chest as I rocked him to and fro. Tears ran down my face to feel his body limp. His arm dropped, lifeless, at his side; hearing a soft thud, I looked down and watched my crystal roll from his open hand. Slowly the realisation dawned: he had looked into the hidden world, but unlike me, he had not returned.

I lay him gently down and rested an ear against his chest. Nothing, and then a soft heartbeat. A long pause, and then another; faint, but there.

'He's alive,' I said.

Juna looked at me, stunned, before bending down to listen for himself. 'I don't understand,' he said. 'I thought…' He watched me pick up the crystal and said, 'What is that? What's wrong with him?'

'I'm not sure,' I said. 'There's no time to explain; I need to try something.'

I turned away to focus on the crystal. If I could get through the gateway, maybe I could find Wanda, maybe I could bring him home. Moments passed and I waited, willing the light to come, willing the mist to reach out and claim me, but the crystal sat in the palm of my hand an inert stone.

I discarded the crystal in my pocket and turned back to Wanda.

'We have to get him to Gogo,' I said, scooping him up in my arms.

I carried Wanda outside where Zandi was waiting. Juna tailed behind on foot, as we raced on horseback over the plains.

Gogo was alone in the hut, stoking the fire, still wearing her nightgown, her hair hanging loose about her shoulders. The calm expression on her face remained unaltered when I entered carrying Wanda, Zandi close behind me.

'He's looked into the crystal,' I said, laying Wanda by the fire. 'He won't wake up.'

I held the crystal out to Gogo; she glanced at it only briefly before turning her gaze to Wanda.

'What crystal?' Zandi said, coming closer to see. Seeing the hurt look on her face, I wished I'd told her about it before.

Gogo pressed her hand against Wanda's forehead and closed her eyes. When she opened them again she turned to me, eyes glistening.

'Fear of the child's gift left me blind,' she said. 'It led Rhonad down a dark path, but I was wrong to fear Wanda.' She reached out for my hand, squeezing my fingers. 'The boy looks to the light. The Mantra has reached out to him, has spoken to him, and Wanda has heard. He is with our Great Spirit.'

I stared at her, eyes wide and said, 'How? Where is he? How can we bring him back?'

Gogo said, 'He has crossed into a place of shadow; a place beyond time, beyond life; the Land Beyond.' She turned to Zandi and said, 'Go gather the elders; tell them to meet us at the graveside.'

'Graveside!' I said, as Zandi left the hut.

'Wanda will need all of our prayers,' Gogo said, 'and the power of the sacred burial site to give strength to our words.' She wrapped her shawl around her shoulders and slowly stood, reaching for the walking stick. 'Come, bring Wanda.'

I followed her, carrying Wanda through the village to the edge of the forest. Just beyond the trees we came to a raised patch of ground, surrounded by a circle of stones. The size of it appeared twice as big as a man's grave.

'Who's buried here?' I asked.

Gogo said, 'Here lie the remains of creatures killed in the massacre on the mountains. The stone circle protects their bones and keeps their spirits safe in the Land Beyond.'

She knelt down on the ground, facing the grave, hands clasped together in front of her face, her eyes closed and head bowed. I lay Wanda on the ground and sat beside him, staring into his face, wondering at the power of his gift, wondering at the power of the crystal that had shown me a glimpse of a spirit world.

The elders arrived in a slow, steady procession, forming a circle around the grave.

'Blessed be the return of the Mantra. Blessed be the return of the rains,' they chanted over and over in a low-pitched chorus.

They were followed by the villagers, the keepers and finally Juna. With Zandi on one side and Juna on the other, I clutched Wanda's hand, listening to the chanting. They were just words; they had only ever just been words, but in a sacred forest where life had survived, seeing Wanda locked in mystery, I felt swayed by the power of prayer.

Gogo slowly stood and addressed the gathering: 'We have waited for this day for many years; we have lived in hope that the Mantra might reach out to us. Our Great Spirit has graced us; it has spoken, and Wanda, a boy gifted to speak the tongues of animals, has heard.'

The elders rocked from side to side, voicing their excitement in hushed whispers: 'Blessed be the return of the Mantra.'

Gogo turned her gaze to me, cool clarity in her eyes as she said, 'You must go to him; you must go to Wanda and hear the Mantra's message.'

I felt the crystal through the fabric of my smock and said, 'But how? The crystal's showing me nothing.'

'Because that gateway is closed,' she said. 'But there's another. For long enough I couldn't make sense of the stones, but now I see. In the oceans of the north, two white rocks rise out of the sea. Day and night they're touched by starlight. It is a gateway between birth and death; a gateway into the Land Beyond; a gateway seen only by those with the power to enter.'

I looked into her eyes, desperate at the thought that what she was suggesting sounded impossible. But her gaze didn't falter.

'But I have no power,' I said. 'Even if I could get there, even if I could find these two white rocks, how do I know I'd see the gateway?'

Gogo said, 'After all this time, all you've seen, do you still doubt you have the gift of a dreamwalker?'

I thought back to all the unanswered questions: my cool appearance in view of the keepers' hidden sense; the strange dream I had had on my journey here, appearing as a ghost alongside myself in the marketplace; the recent dream of Wanda, that had felt like so much more than a dream; and the familiar cold that connected me to my mother, and to the mist.

Gogo said, 'The Mantra sees all; the past, present and future. It sees those who believe, and among us it sees those who are gifted. It saw you, and your mother, and the crystal that connected you, and through the crystal it reached out to Wanda. This has always been a quest of many threads and now it's down to you, a dreamwalker who *will* see the gateway into the Land Beyond, a gateway formed from the mists of *Serafay*.'

'I'm sorry, Gogo,' Zandi said. 'But what you're suggesting... Even if Suni is gifted like you say, just how is she supposed to find this place in the middle of the sea?'

'Look how far she's already come,' Gogo said, 'how far the quest has come.' She turned to look at me, a solemn look in her eyes as she said, 'We must have hope and we must have faith.'

I looked down at Wanda and thought of my dream, imagined him locked into a world, a world that the wise woman believed I could find. I had come so far with my young companion, a boy I'd long loved as kin. I couldn't leave him now. If an enchanted gateway existed, any ship would surely know about it, and a crystal the size of mine would be plenty to pay for passage. But the thought of travelling by merchant ship was an unsavoury one; most were sailed by pirates. Only the rafts were safe, but they only came in the summer months. After my years in the mountain, and seeing weeks of rain in the valley, I'd lost track of the seasons.

I looked at Gogo and asked, 'What season are we in?'

'The rains bring the start of summer,' she said.

I nodded and said, 'I might know a way, although I can't be sure the rafts dock at Shendi anymore.'

The Gogo smiled and said, 'I think the tides will be with you.'

I saw her unwavering faith and looked away, unsettled by the prospect of returning to my hometown.

Juna put his hand on my shoulder and said, 'I'll come with you as far as the estuary. I know a way that avoids the town.'

I was grateful for the understanding I saw in his eyes, and asked, 'Have you been there?'

'I've been far enough to see it,' he said. 'There are cliffs west of here that drop down to desert, and streams following north to the estuary. But it'll take days on foot.'

'Horses will take you as far as the gorge,' Zandi said.

I leaned over Wanda and whispered in his ear, 'I'm coming for you.'

Chapter 29

The horse rode hard across the plains, until we were travelling beneath a cloudless sky. I looked ahead, seeing the ground blanketed by a shimmery haze; stray wisps of mist travelled south with the breeze. The horse came to an abrupt stop, not willing to tread where the scent of death lingered. From there Juna led the way on foot, approaching the cliff edge where the view below was revealed.

Desert on one side, grasslands on the other; the cliffs provided a dramatic boundary between the two extremes. Further north, we came to the gorge: a great rocky chasm where sporadic vegetation sprouted from the rocks. The sun was setting, casting shadows around the gorge as we climbed down; by the time we reached sand, it was almost dark.

'We'll camp here tonight,' Juna said, gathering dry bush into a pile.

I watched the smouldering flames take hold, listened to the crackling of burning grass break the silence of the desert.

Over a supper of bread and cheese I said, 'I'm glad you're here, Juna. I don't think I could have faced this journey on my own.'

'I want Wanda back as well,' he said.

'I know you do. I think he looks at you like a father. You've taken such good care of him.'

'Not good enough.'

'No, this is my fault,' I said. 'If only I'd hidden the crystal from him…'

'A crystal? You were in the mines,' he said.

I nodded, avoiding his eye.

'What you've seen in the crystal,' he said at last, 'the place Wanda is... Is it like a dream?'

'It feels like a dream, I guess. But it isn't. It's hard to explain.'

'It's like Wanda with the animals,' he said. 'I can splint an owl's leg, but only Wanda can give it the will to live. He talks to them in a tongue I don't understand, but that doesn't make it any less true. Perhaps it's the same with the Mantra, and a gateway in the sea that will take you into the Land Beyond.'

'I only hope I can find him,' I said.

'You have to,' he said, staring into the flames. He leaned forward, and tossed a few bundles of brush onto the fire. 'All the stories my mother told me as a child, of the forest, at the time I thought they were just that, stories. And maybe they were, but then again, maybe *she* believed in the Mantra.'

I reached for a stick and joined Juna in stoking the fire.

'It's strange for me,' I said, 'to know that you come from the palace, to think that there were people there, of all places, telling stories of wildlife in the time before the drought.' I poked at the flames. 'All I knew about the palace was from stories and rumours passed around town, and the annual plays performed at the festival, when the King would arrive with his face covered. The townspeople believe the palace is an enchanted place. They think that the Earth Spirit Orag, looks out through the King's eyes, giving him the power to turn people to sand just by gazing at them, a power he once used against a rebellion. My mother never believed any of it; she always said they were lies told to keep people away from the palace, so the King could hold onto power and keep control over the crystals. She always said that Orag, doesn't exist. I paused. 'But now Gogo said it does.'

Juna said, 'We grew the King's food, cooked for him, looked after his goats and camels, but we never laid eyes on him. I never heard of the King having the power to turn people to sand, or of an attempt to overthrow him. I grew up fearing my father, not the King.'

'So my mother was right,' I said. 'A lie told by the palace to keep people afraid, to keep people away.'

'Maybe,' Juna said. 'The only time the men spoke to the women and children was to give orders, or hand out punishment. We only knew what we overheard, and I don't remember much talk about the King. But I did know about Orag, everyone did. It was a vague story passed around in whispers that had as many versions as tellers.' He lapsed into silence, and stared at the flames. Quietly, he added, 'I remember once, I must have only been about four or five. It was the first time my father beat me, the first time I learnt to fear him.' His voice grew hard. 'After the first lash of his belt hit my back, I shouted at him, "Orag will come for you!" I had no idea what it meant, no idea what the consequences would be for yelling at my father. Just before he beat me black and blue, and beat my mother for trying to pull him off me, I remember, just for a moment, my father looked afraid. Who knows, maybe Gogo's right, and maybe there was something my father was afraid of after all.'

'If she is right,' I said, 'then the return of the Mantra would save us from more than a drought.'

I woke at sunrise, stiff from a restless sleep, to find Juna scouring the ground just beyond the mouth of the gorge. Faint lines in the ground, where the sand was darker, signified underground streams. We followed them north, where shallow rivulets formed above ground, criss-crossing until they widened into a stream. The widening tributary, the sight of reeds, was the only change in an otherwise stark landscape, as we embarked on a three day trek. The nights brought refreshing relief from the hot sun, and the company of desert mice; the only signs of life.

By the morning of the third day, the stream had claimed status as a river. As the afternoon wore on, the eastern horizon was slowly changing. I looked out, tasting bile in the back of my throat as the town came into view. Juna put his hand on my shoulder and kept it there, as the sound of voices drifted downstream towards us.

'Someone might recognise me,' I quietly said.

'I doubt it,' Juna said. 'It was a long time ago. In any case, look at us; we look like beggars.'

Glancing up at the sun, I said, 'The market will be closing soon. If the raft people are here, they'll head back to the rafts for the night.'

I kept my head down as we passed fishermen reining in their catch, and women rinsing washing. Further on, where the river widened to meet the estuary, we saw canoes moored on the banks. The seascape stretched out before us, and there, beyond the waves, I saw the rafts in the distance. Gogo was right; the tides were with us.

'It's the first time I've seen the sea,' Juna said.

His expression was a mixture of awe and fear. I had been glad of his company, but knew, from here, I would be going on alone.

We sat down on the bank, a safe distance from the townspeople further downstream, and kept a watchful eye out for the raft people. The more time passed, the more anxious I became.

'I don't remember the raft people being interested in crystals,' I said. 'What if they don't let me board?'

'We'll soon find out,' Juna said, eyes on a young man approaching.

Looking at the weary expression on the young man's face, and the fish draped over his shoulder, I whispered to Juna, 'He hasn't sold his catch. Those fish were caught at sea.'

'Are you selling those?' Juna called to the man.

'What they worth to you?' the man said.

Juna beckoned me ahead and followed close behind.

I took the crystal from my pocket and held it out to show the man, pleased to see his eyes widen.

'This crystal and passage on the rafts,' I said.

'Passage to where?' he said, not taking his eyes off the crystal.

'North,' I said. 'Where two white rocks stand out from the sea.'

He looked at me, eyes narrowed and said, 'The rafts won't go there. That place is cursed.'

I closed my fingers around the crystal and went to put it back in my pocket.

'Wait,' the man said. 'I'll trade you for the fish.'

'No deal,' Juna said.

'Why do you want to go there?' he asked.

'That's my business,' I said. 'Do you want the crystal, or not?'

'My father will. I'll take you aboard; you'll have to see what he says.'

Juna looked at me, eyebrows raised in a question. I shrugged and gave an uneasy smile.

'I'll wait here,' Juna said to me. 'If you're not back today, I'll see you at the gorge.' He turned to the man. 'She'll go with you. I'll have the fish.'

I climbed down into the canoe, and, with Juna watching from the banks, we paddled out into open sea.

Chapter 30

I had never been afraid of the ocean; it made no sense to me to fear a place where others happily lived. But sailing out into open waters with only a humble canoe keeping us afloat, I kept my eyes fixed on the approaching rafts, eager to reach them.

Up close, the rafts were an intriguing sight, bigger and more sophisticated than I had imagined. Individual rafts topped with wooden huts, interlinked by a complex causeway of walkways and rope bridges, created a town on water, sturdy against the drifting tides. The outer rafts were busy with people gutting fish, mending nets, and hauling in the catch. One by one they looked up from what they were doing, watching as our canoe approached.

'What on the great seas are you doing, Tanvier?' one woman shouted down. 'Who is this woman?'

'Where's my father?' Tanvier said, climbing up onto the raft. 'I need to speak to him.' He turned back to me, reaching down to take my hand. 'You coming?'

I took his hand and climbed aboard, nervous to find myself face to face with the woman. She wiped bloodied hands on her apron before embedding them into plump hips, and all the while watching me with a distinctly unwelcoming expression.

She turned to Tanvier and said, 'What you doing bringing a land dweller aboard?'

'Let her past, Samira,' he said, taking my arm and pulling me through the growing crowd. 'Father!' he shouted. He led me to a man with a dark bushy beard, a cap worn low over his eyes, and his mouth set into a grim line. 'She wants passage,' Tanvier said to his father. He nudged my arm and said to me, 'Show him.'

When I held up the crystal, the man's jaw relaxed and his eyes widened at the sight of it.

'Passage to where?' he said.

'North,' I said. 'Where two white rocks stand out from the water.'

He reached up, pushing back the cap on his head and said, 'Why there?'

'My business is my own,' I said.

'That place is cursed,' Samira said. 'Send her back, Babacus.'

It was a sentiment shared among the crowd, but Babacus had eyes fixed on the crystal.

'The seas aren't what they used to be,' he said, in a voice loud enough for everyone to hear. 'This crystal will pay for protection against pirates.' He looked at me, held out his hand and said, 'We'll take you. But you must have a death wish.'

'Babacus!' Samira said. 'Ships have been lost between those rocks!'

Babacus held the crystal up to the sun and said, 'We'll take her close enough to paddle a canoe. If she wants to take her chances, that's up to her.' He tucked the crystal safely into his jacket pocket and strode off, shouting, 'Pull the anchors! Hoist the masts! We sail north!'

Some in the crowd lingered, arguing amongst themselves. I knew the raft people to be superstitious, believing in the spirits of the land and sea; seeing their fear of my destination left me unnerved.

As the rafts set sail, I edged away from the crowd onto an adjoining raft, and sat among barrels of dried meat and spices. My destination and the fact I was a land dweller meant I was unpopular and left alone.

A woman passed by on the adjoining raft, carrying a bucket hooked in the crux of her arm. She was watching me, eyes gently squinting, as though confused. I looked back; the sight of her face seemed oddly familiar. Her mouth fell open; she dropped the bucket, fish heads spilling out over the deck. Slowly she crossed the bridge that separated us. My stomach was churning, my skin turned clammy. *Nisrin?* It couldn't be, and yet the woman looked just like her. I couldn't move, couldn't believe my eyes.

'Suni?' she said, coming to stand in front of me, her eyes open wide in disbelief. 'Is it really you?'

'Nisrin?' I whispered, my face crumpled in confusion as I slowly stood up to face her.

'How?' She reached out, tentatively touching my face. 'We thought you were dead?'

She rested her hands on my shoulders then pulled me into her chest. I stood awkwardly in her embrace, arms hanging limp at my sides. I had lived with ghosts for so many years; now my thoughts raced back in time, trying to make sense of the confusion.

I felt her mouth press against my ear, heard her whisper, 'Suni, your mother is here.'

I stood back to see her face, held onto her arms to steady myself against the feeling of dizziness. I stared into her eyes, wondering why she would say that to me, but there was no lie in her eyes; she was the same Nisrin I remembered.

The dizziness subsided, leaving me numb as, with eyes fixed on hers I said, 'I don't understand, I thought you were dead. I thought my mother was dead.'

The sun was shining but I shivered with cold, as I sank down onto a barrel. Nisrin took off her shawl and wrapped it around my shoulders, then sat down next to me, one hand resting over mine. I stared down at the raft, focused on the grains patterned in the wood.

'She was in the house,' I whispered. 'You were both in the house. I left early, and when I came back, the house was on fire, with you barricaded inside.'

Nisrin gripped my hand and said, 'We weren't in the house. We'd left before sunrise while you were still sleeping. Mata went off to run an errand while I came back to the rafts for more stock. On my way back to shore I saw Mata swimming out to the rafts. She was screaming, saying they'd burnt the house down with you in it; she almost drowned. Neither one of us have stepped on land since.'

The house was empty...

Nisrin stood up, pulling at my hand, and said, 'Come with me. I'll take you to your mother.'

I followed as though in a trance, across walkways and bridges deep into the rafts. I saw the brightly-painted huts, smelt fish frying, sights, sounds and smells that seemed strangely distant. She stopped outside a hut, where a tapestry hung over the door; it was a design I recognised as Mata's.

I stepped inside the darkened room and saw a woman sitting at a loom, working the comb and needle by dim lantern light. Her fingers slowed to a stop when she looked up and met my eyes, a long lingering look that saw the years unravel. I felt the silent tears roll down my face, but Mata's face remain unchanged as she reached her hand out to me. Slowly I walked towards her, sank to my knees, dropped my head in her lap and cried.

She sat silently stroking my hair, while the years of grief fell away like shattered glass. As my cries subsided, I buried my face in the folds of her smock, breathed in the scent of her musty smell, and slowly lifted my head to face her. Up close I saw her sunken eyes and protruding cheekbones. She appeared frail, but there was strength in her shining eyes.

She reached out to touch my hair and said, 'For so many years, I thought my daughter was dead.'

She raised a handkerchief to her mouth when she coughed, dry and rasping. I sat up, and put a hand on her shoulder, feeling the sharp lines of her bones. Nisrin came forward with a spoonful of syrup, and slowly the coughing subsided. Mata dabbed the corners of her mouth with the handkerchief, before stuffing it into her cupped hand.

'You're ill,' I said, running my other hand down her arm, realising how loosely her clothes were hanging over her thin frame.

She shook her head, rested a hand on my cheek and leaned forward to kiss me on the forehead. When she sat back I gazed into her eyes, confused to see how calm she appeared, as though she had been expecting me.

'You look so grown up,' she said. 'How did you survive?'

How to tell her I'd gone to the mines, the source of the King's power, to look for the man that had betrayed her? After everything, I couldn't bear her to think that I had betrayed her too. As a child I'd known her to be strong and resilient, inflexible in her doctrine. But she was not the same woman, and I was no longer a girl. And so I told her about my years living as a boy and my hopes for my father, and she listened without judgement.

'I thought I'd seen your ghost,' I said, as I spoke about seeing her apparition in the crystal cave, and again in the mist held within the crystal. 'I thought you were watching over me, reaching out to me.'

She said, 'After I thought you'd died, my vision of you grew clearer. Seeing you in that dark place, I thought you'd found no peace in death. I wanted to bring you light.'

'You did,' I said. 'In the crystal.'

She slowly nodded and said, 'It broke my heart to think of you so alone.'

'I wasn't alone,' I said.

When I told of Wanda she clasped her hands to her face, smiling to hear of his meetings with mice in the middle of the night. I avoided telling her of the brothel, instead recounting how Fazi had helped me escape to the valley beyond the mountains. Hearing about my father she gave nothing away, but when I described the valley she leaned forward, eyes wide.

'My grandmother?' she said. 'You've met my grandmother.'

'She is called Gogo now.'

She looked on proudly when I told of my training to be a keeper, gripped my hand when I explained about spells woven from out of the abyss. Light shone in her eyes to know that all she had once fought for still existed; more than she ever imagined. But when I told of Wanda falling prey to the crystal, locked in the Land Beyond, her gaze drifted to stare into space.

'Mata?' I said.

Moments passed before finally her eyes rested back on mine.

'So many years I thought you were dead, and I grieved for you. Until I saw something that gave me hope you were still alive.'

'Mata?' Nisrin said from the corner. 'What do you mean?'

Mata looked towards her friend and said, 'It was a hope I didn't dare speak out loud. I've seen Suni in the mists at the edge of my dreams for many years, but a gift can be confused with desire.'

'You're talking about dreamwalking,' I said.

She turned to face me, eyebrows raised.

'Gogo calls them the mists of *Serafay*,' I said. 'Mists that the dead or a dreamwalker can know.'

She nodded and said, 'I thought it was through my gift as a seer that I could see your spirit, until I saw you looking into the dream of the boy you call Wanda.' 'You were there?' I said. 'I looked for you, in the mist, but I didn't see you.'

'You were drawn to the boy,' she said, 'and that led you to his dream. I followed you, I saw you try to reach him, and then you were gone.'

'I couldn't reach him,' I said.

'Because the boy's dream is no ordinary dream,' she said, 'and the Land Beyond is a place not visible to the eyes of the living. '

'But I saw it,' I said. 'I saw a dying forest, and Wanda there, among the trees.'

She nodded and said, 'And now you're on a journey to save the boy.'

I told of Gogo's prophecy: without the return of the Mantra, we faced a breaking of the world. Once Mata would have denied the existence of Orag, but hearing it came from Gogo, she listened without question.

'All my years on Shendi, I thought I knew what we were fighting against,' she said. 'But I was wrong. The resistance survived, and with them the truth survived. But I wasn't wrong about you, my daughter. You are the hope for the future. But you can't do this alone.'

'Gogo said the mists of *Serafay* form a gateway to the Land Beyond,' I said. 'She said a dreamwalker can pass through.'

Mata nodded and said, 'A dreamwalker can enter, but that won't help you find your way.'

Her chest heaved and she began coughing again. When she lowered her hand I saw drops of blood smeared on the handkerchief. I reached over and took it from her.

Mata put her hand on mine and said, 'I've had fever in my chest for a year or more. I'm dying, Suni.'

I shook my head and said, 'You're sick; we can find a way to make you well. There are healers in the valley, and Gogo. She'd know a way.'

She shook her head and said, 'It's the reason I could see what the boy saw, what was hidden from you; the colours of the spirit world. It's the reason I can help you find Wanda. You can enter the mist, but the Land Beyond will appear only as shadows to you. Without my help you won't find your way. The boy doesn't belong there; I can help you bring him home.'

'No, Mata,' Nisrin said. 'If you enter the spirit world you won't return.'

Mata looked at her friend, smiled and said, 'Whether I go now, or later, you know I don't have long.'

Nisrin quietly held my mother's gaze before she lowered her head and left the hut.

'I can't lose you again,' I said, my voice breaking. 'I need you.'

Mata put her arms around me, pressed my head into her chest, and said, 'I thought that was true once. But you're so strong, and you've made me proud. Wanda needs you, and our homeland needs you.' I locked my arms around her waist as she gently rocked me from side to side. 'You remember the stories I used to tell you, and how we dreamed of seeing the rains return. You've seen so much already, and now you can show me. To see forest up close is more than I could have hoped for.'

Staring into the lantern light, I said, 'How can I lose you again?'

'You just ... let me go,' Mata said.

Huddled with my mother, I watched the lantern until the light flickered out.

Chapter 31

Morning came, grey and drizzling over choppy seas. Hearing the call for anchors to drop, my heart was pounding with the thought I would lose my mother, again. Families watched our sombre procession to the outer rafts, and gathered in behind as the rafts ground to a stop, curious to see the mystical gateway they all feared. It was just as Gogo had said: a star shone bright over two tall peaks of white rock rising up from the ocean.

Mata's body was frail but there was strength in her eyes as she clasped Nisrin's face in her hands and smiled.

'Goodbye dearest friend,' Mata said, gently pulling Nisrin's face towards her and kissing her on the forehead.

Mata turned to me, one eyebrow raised as she held out her hand. I helped my mother down into the canoe and, with a heavy heart, picked up the paddles. Nisrin wiped the tears from her eyes and forced a smile, as she waved her friend off on her final journey.

The drizzling rain washed away my tears as I paddled away from the rafts. My mother was in front, her back to me as she gazed ahead at the rocks. I was torn, desperate to turn back and keep her with me, while needing to go on, to see Wanda safely home again. My mother was dying, but no amount of frailty could mask the strength of her convictions. In her presence I felt like a child again. Her silence drove me on, her steely determination gave strength to my arms as I paddled the choppy waters. I followed the line of her gaze, eyes resting on the rocks, anticipating a gateway of mist. But there was no sign of enchantment, other than starlight glistening against the white rocks.

'Keep us steady,' Mata said, seeing we were drifting off course.

She reached back to take hold of a paddle and dug into the water as if she were as young as me. Shocked, I dragged the other paddle through the waves, but already the canoe was back on course.

Approaching the rocks, the water grew completely calm. Mata stopped paddling and leaned back, reaching out to put a hand over mine. The canoe continued gliding forwards on its own, swept along on a current that took us into the channelling water between the rocks.

I looked up at the steep splintering walls either side. On our approach, they had appeared as two singular rocks surrounded by ocean, but as we moved along, the walls stretched out before us to form a tunnel. Realising the rain had stopped, I looked up at the sky. A sudden bright white light dazzled down, reflecting all around the walls. I cupped a hand to my forehead to shield my eyes.

The light faded as suddenly as it had appeared, leaving us looking out into thick mist. The canoe drifted forwards through calm waters to where the mist slowly cleared, revealing a strange world: the world from my dream, the Land Beyond. Beneath a dull grey sky the current carried us along a snaking river, through a lifeless forest of gnarled blackened trees with bare branches. I looked at my mother, saw her gaze into the forest with eager eyes, knowing colours were revealed to her that were hidden from me.

'Over there,' Mata said, dipping the paddle into the water and steering us towards the bank.

She sounded different, her voice echoing, distant and detached. Reaching the water's edge, she climbed out of the canoe, her body now nimble and spry. I climbed out after, kept my eyes fixed on her, frightened as her skin paled to ashen grey. She led the way into the trees, sure-footed on uneven ground littered with fallen branches and exposed roots.

I tripped over a vine and stumbled, reaching out to grab hold of a tree to break my fall. I glimpsed something above me move on the lifeless bark, just beyond my reach, and looked up to see. Camouflaged against the tones of grey, I caught a fleeting glance of something long and slender dart out of sight; I wondered if it was a lizard.

I stood back from the tree and looked around, seeing my mother further on up the path. Afraid of this eerie world, I ran to catch up with her. As she walked, she gazed all around, into the bush, peering up at trees. We were surrounded by what appeared to be shadows merging with the undergrowth, fleeting glimpses of what I thought were wings, a tusk, a tail. I reached for Mata's arm. Her skin felt cool.

'What are they?' I asked, motioning outward, sensing she already belonged to this world.

'Spirits of the creatures of our homeland,' she said, smiling as she spoke in the same distant voice. 'The Mantra is here, and your boy is here.'

Seeing the joy on her face as she led me along, I remembered the first time I had seen the sacred forest and all the wildlife that lived there. The colour of life in the Land Beyond was hidden from me, but I saw it reflected in my mother's eyes. That she was content and happy was a comfort. All she had fought for was within reach, and she would see it.

We came to the end of the trees, where the ground rose up into a rocky hillside. The shadowy creatures of the forest melted back into the undergrowth, but among the rocks and boulders of the slopes, more creatures gathered. I looked among the shadowy forms as they moved, seeing feline characteristics as they stretched and arched their backs. My mother turned to face me, smiling as she looked at me with wide eyes; I smiled back to see her looking youthful. The colours of her skin and clothes were blending with the greys of this world. She started up the slope, climbing easily over rocks and boulders, making her pilgrimage to the mountain lions.

Standing alone at the foot of the hillside I felt adrift, until a wisp of cool breeze brushed the back of my neck. I turned and saw Wanda standing behind me.

'I knew you'd come,' he said, his voice sounding distant like Mata's.

He appeared as an apparition, rich in colours that contrasted with the spirit world.

I knelt down to face him and said, 'I've come to find a way to bring you home, Wanda. You don't belong here.'

'The gateway closed behind me,' he said.

'I know,' I said. 'Tell me what I can do.'

Wanda turned to look back at the forest. I followed his gaze and saw the branches of trees gently sway as though a breeze was stirring. The sound of rustling leaves filled the air, even though, to my eyes, the trees were dead and bare. When the forest fell silent, Wanda looked back at me and opened his mouth. A voice spoke through him, sounding like a chorus of many voices pitched high and low:

'Your people waged war against the creatures of my realm, and even in death they are insulted. Your rulers hang their heads on the palace walls like trophies, and feel nothing but pride for the murders. Your elders offer their prayers, asking for forgiveness. I hear their words, but their words are too few among your people. I could return, I could restore the rains and bring life back to the desert. But I will not deliver life just to face another massacre.'

'What can I do?' I said. 'What can our world do to set things right?'

'Deliver proof,' the voice said. 'Proof that the resistance can stand against the killers, proof that they have more than words. The head of the first mountain lion your King killed hangs on the palace wall. Take back the head, lay it alongside the rest of its remains; give peace to its spirit. Do this, and I will make peace with your land, and return your boy.'

As the voice faded, so too did the image of Wanda. I reached out but my hands touched only air and Wanda was gone.

Something cool touched my shoulder. I turned to see my mother standing behind me; her bodily form diminished. She appeared as a ghost.

She smiled and said, 'Go home, Suni; deliver the Mantra's message to our people and you will see Wanda again.' She looked behind me, into the trees. 'You must leave, there's not much time.'

The forest was creaking and groaning. I turned to see branches of trees arching, twisting, leaning towards neighbouring trees to form archways. Vines coiled upwards and outwards from tree trunks, weaving patterns in the air as they twisted together, closing the path. I looked back for my mother, and felt a lump in my throat to see her gone. Alone in this eerie world, I ran for the path.

The trees moved and formed behind my every step as I ran for the river. I didn't look back, just ran as fast as my legs could go, fearing the forest was trying to ensnare me. I reached the canoe and pushed off, only pausing to glance back once I was clear of the bank. Realising the canoe was gliding back downstream toward shore, I pushed back against the current. Watched by shadows from the trees, I paddled upstream towards the wall of mist.

As the tip of the canoe touched the mist, I felt a gust of wind from behind and paused mid-stroke of the paddles. I slowly turned, curious of the reason for the change in the air, and was met by a miraculous sight. A creature stepped out of the forest, watching me from the bank. Standing as tall as the trees it was full in bodily form, with curious features, richly-coloured: the brown body of a deer; a long neck covered with a yellow mane; and a black face like a monkey, with dashes of white around its eyes and bristles of red hair on its chin. Every branch it touched, and the ground beneath its yellowed two-toed hooves, burst with newly sprouting leaf that withered when it moved on. Locked in its gaze I felt its power: as strong as a raging storm, as tender as the gentlest breeze, and as curious as a child's first view of the world. And yet for all its power it lowered its neck as though bowing. When it raised its head, it turned back into the trees. As it did I saw its face transform before my eyes, from monkey to deer to wolf to eagle – the Mantra, a Great Spirit with ever changing faces.

Chapter 32

The mist came and went. The boat rocking on choppy waters, cool rain on my face, the strong smell of sea air, all came like a sudden awakening from a dream. I gripped the paddles and pushed down into the water, eyes looking beyond the rocks tipped with starlight. There was no sign of a gateway, no hint of a hidden world. The Mantra had given me hope, but now I was alone in the boat.

Nisrin was waiting for me at the edge of the raft where I had left her, and she wasn't alone. On the journey out, the raft people had been reluctant in offering me passage, but on my return from the Land Beyond, I saw their feeling towards me had changed. They were a nomadic people, respectful of the natural world above all else, and hearing I had been in the presence of the Mantra, now they welcomed me as their guest, eager to know of the spirited world, and the wildlife of a hidden valley.

In return I learnt about their nomadic life at sea following migrating shoals, and watched fearless young children swim far out from the rafts among wildlife I'd never seen before: turtles, dolphins, whales and many more extraordinary creatures. Life aboard the rafts appeared free and simple: a community of people respecting their environment and grateful for all it provided. I thought about Shendi's history in times before the King, nomadic tribes living in harmony with the land. The Mantra had set the terms for its return, but even if we succeeded, what would the future hold? The King's reign had wrought ruin upon our land. As the rafts sailed steadily south I let my mind drift, dreaming of a future where the people of Shendi might be free from the King's tyranny and lies.

The midday sun beat down from a clear sky when the shores of Shendi appeared on the horizon. After thanking my gracious hosts, I set off with Nisrin to shore, our boat escorted by five other canoes intending to mask my arrival. Staggered stops were made along the riverbank, the last canoe following us beyond the fishermen to where the river was quiet. I said my heartfelt goodbyes to Nisrin, watched her climb into her neighbour's canoe and turn upstream, then I picked up the paddles, eager to put the town behind me.

The gentle splashing of the paddles, water lapping against the bow of the boat, were welcomed distractions on my lonely journey through the desert. A night passed, and the river shallowed to stream. Another night passed and the stream branched into arteries that soon ran dry in the barren land. On foot I dragged the canoe behind, too afraid to leave it behind in case it was found. When I thought my arms could take no more, I dropped it and sat down to rest. Sipping at my flask, chewing the last morsel of dried fish, I squinted against the bright sun, looking into the eastern horizon. The shimmering haze of dry heat revealed colours of the cliffs.

After an exhausting journey, I was relieved at the sight of Juna in the gorge roasting fish over a fire. As I told of the extraordinary revelations from the Land Beyond, he listened in silence, a sombre look on his face. He left me eating a fish supper, while he set to work burning the canoe. Watching his silhouette in the glow of the fire, feeling the silence stretch out between us, I could only imagine the trepidation he felt at the thought of returning to the palace.

The prospect of how the keepers would take the news was one we both mulled over as we journeyed on to the forest. Without their help, our quest had little chance of success. When finally we arrived, we found Gogo where we had left her; still wearing her nightgown, she sat among the elders keeping vigil over Wanda.

'You saw your mother,' Gogo said to me, reaching for my hand.

I nodded and glanced at the stones scattered beside her, before resting my eyes on Wanda. Seeing the peaceful look on his sleeping face, I imagined the Mantra watching over him in a distant world.

Before long, villagers and keepers joined the gathering, and silence fell as I told of my journey. When I finished speaking, the elders raised their hands in the air, chanting in unison as they recited the familiar prayer. But I kept my eye on the keepers, watched some turn to leave, and saw, among those that remained, familiar scepticism.

Chad came forward and said, 'It's not for me to say what you did or didn't see, but what you're asking can't be done. You must know that.' When I didn't answer he looked to Juna and said, '*You* know it better than anyone. We'd be outnumbered, on unfamiliar territory; revealing our weakness to the enemy is suicide for all of us.'

'The keepers have defended us for many years,' Gogo said, 'risking their lives day and night. But I tell you this; without the return of the Mantra, then Orag will wake, and if that day comes, there will be no land, and no people left to defend.'

I looked among the keepers, fearing that the quest would fail before it had begun; they no more believed in a breaking of the world than the existence of the Mantra. I turned to Zandi, walked towards her and reached for her hands.

'Please, Zandi,' I said. 'It's the only way.'

'I know what Wanda means to you,' she said. 'But what you're asking, it's impossible.'

'It's not me asking,' I said. 'I saw the Mantra with my own eyes. I heard it with my own ears. No words could tell you how extraordinary and powerful it is. It *is* real, and its connection to this land is real. I once told you about where I come from, a barren desert; if we don't do this, you'll see the same here, we all will. The Mantra wants to return, to breathe life into the land. You may not believe in prophecies, you may not believe in Orag, but I'm asking you to believe in me.'

She reached up to brush my cheek and said, 'You look so different.'

I looked into her eyes, saw her eyebrows gently furrow, as she turned to Juna and asked, 'Only you know the palace, Juna. What do you think?'

'The men in the palace outnumber you,' he said. 'But they don't have your skill, and an attack is the last thing they'd be expecting. From what I remember, come evening they'll be too drunk to put up any real defence.'

Zandi looked back at me, eyes gently squinting, before she turned to face the keepers and said, 'Whether we believe in the Mantra or not, I believe in Suni. We've all seen how different she looks to our other sense; none of us can explain what can only be a gift. She's seen things, I can see it on her face, and I trust her. Imagine if she's right and we do nothing.'

'I'm with you,' Nita said, turning to look at me. 'You're one of us, a comrade; you've trained with us, worked with us, watched our backs and trusted us to watch yours. I don't believe you'd put any one of us in danger if there was another way.'

Bindi came forward to stand beside her sister, and said, 'Juna knows the palace. I say we get in and get the lion's head out. We'll take them all out if we have to.'

As resolve slowly rippled among the group, Juna said, 'We cross the border on the eastern ridge.'

Chapter 33

It was dusk by the time our band of twenty keepers set up camp for the night, high in the mountain foothills. I sat with Zandi as we watched Juna head off alone up the pass.

'We're relying on him,' Zandi said. 'Do you think he'll be okay?'

'He'll do what he has to, for Wanda's sake,' I said.

'Did he tell you why he ran away from the palace?' she asked, turning to look at me.

I met her eye and said, 'It's for Juna to talk about.'

She nodded, lowered her eyes and said, 'You're close to Juna.'

'He saved Wanda's life,' I said, reaching for her hand, 'and gave us shelter. He's a good friend, but no, I'm not close to him like I am with you.'

'So why didn't you tell me about the crystal?'

I looked down, weaving my fingers between hers and said, 'I don't really know. Maybe I thought you wouldn't believe me. I wasn't even sure what I believed. I'd spent my life running and searching and looking for ways to make my mother proud. Meeting you, training with the keepers, at the time it seemed to make more sense than anything else. For the first time I felt I was in charge of my own destiny.'

'What about now,' she said, 'after seeing your mother again?'

I leaned forward to rest my elbows on my knees and said, 'I keep thinking how different my life would have been if I'd known she was alive, and whether she'd still be alive today if we hadn't been separated in the first place. For so many years I thought I was seeing her ghost; I thought she'd come to watch over me, guide me. That's the only thing that kept me going in the mountains. Now it's hard to know how to feel. Everything started with the fire. It's the reason I left, what led me to the crystal, what brought me to Wanda, to you, to Gogo. It's the reason we're here, right now, trying to save Wanda, and even see the Mantra back here where it belongs.'

Zandi lay back, clasped her hands behind her head and said, 'I always thought the Mantra was just people needing to believe in something bigger than themselves, looking for something to give their lives meaning. But after everything you've said, how can I not believe it?'

I leaned over and kissed her. She wrapped her arms around my neck and pulled me in closer. Believer or not, her presence gave me strength.

At first light our convoy headed towards the pass between two flat-topped crags. Only stray mist lingered; still the keepers, expert horse handlers, had to coax the horses through to the other side. There the keepers saw their first view of the desert; a sombre sight in contrast to the world they knew.

Travelling in the cool of night, with Juna navigating the stars, it was in the early hours of dawn on the third day, rounding a sweeping dune, when we finally glimpsed the palace: a huge sandstone fortress, monstrous, rising out of the sand. Creeping over the dunes we closed in, climbing up a sandy ridge to look out over the palace.

Level with the fortress walls I saw they were topped with a curious collection of stone sculpted heads: wolves, lions, eagles and deer all looking out with lifeless eyes over the surrounding desert. I glanced across at Juna, unsettled by the thought I might be looking at what inspired his own wood carvings.

'We should wait until nightfall,' Juna said, staring straight ahead. 'And go over the eastern wall. Across the grounds, there's a side entrance into the palace. After dark the grounds that side should be clear. Guards only patrol the main gates in the western wall at night, or at least they used to.'

'What about inside the palace?' Chad asked.

'We make for the hallways,' Juna said. 'I don't know where the lion skull is so we'll just have to search. We might get lucky and not be seen. The palace never sleeps, but most of the men will be in the south wing in the dining chambers, or upstairs in the bedrooms.' He paused, rubbing a hand over his mouth. 'Once we're over the wall, we've got to go through the huts where the women and children live. And in the palace, there'll be mistresses, just girls.'

I put a hand on his shoulder and said, 'Why go through the huts? Surely we'd risk being seen.'

He looked at me and said, 'That side is the only way over without being seen by the palace: a wall separates the huts from the rest of the grounds.' He turned to Chad and added, 'The women and children are in bed by sun down, and, in any case, they have no loyalty to the men who hold them prisoner.'

Chad nodded and said, 'The women and children might be innocent, but your father's a guard. If we get caught up with him, we won't hesitate to take him down.'

Juna turned away to look back at the palace, and said, 'I wouldn't stand in your way. I know who my father is.'

Throughout the day we took turns to rest, while others kept watch. I woke feeling the creeping chill of the evening air, and saw the full moon in the night sky. Among the keepers readying to leave, Yuba was standing still, gazing east.

'What is that?' he said, in a low voice.

I turned to see an opaque wall slowly closing in on us.

'It's a sandstorm,' I said. 'And it's heading this way. We'll have to wait till it passes: we won't see anything in that.'

'Where's Juna?' Chad said.

I looked around, seeing Zandi was also missing. I climbed the ridge, found her asleep, and gently woke her.

'Juna's missing,' I said, seeing we were alone on the ridge. I turned to look out at the palace, eyes resting on a dark figure scaling the wall.

'What's he doing?' Zandi said.

'Looking for his mother,' I said. 'I should have realised. Come on, we've got to go after him now, ahead of that.' I pointed at the coming storm.

With the sandstorm drifting slowly towards us, we made our approach on foot, gathering at the eastern wall. Nothing stirred from the other side. Ropes were thrown, anchored around stone heads; silently we scaled to the top, peering out over a mass of dilapidated huts. I was unprepared for the rancid air filled with the stench of latrines and stale cooking odours, shocked to see such cramped dwellings huddled in the shadow of the palace. I looked towards the high wall separating the rest of the palace grounds; even from our vantage point we couldn't see what was on the other side.

We scaled down, silent and alert to the close proximity of the huts. Chad signalled for me to follow and led the way, just the two of us, to search the area for Juna. We moved through the narrow tracks, arrows poised, hearing the sound of soft snoring, babies whimper, and padding feet through the thin walls of these desperate dwellings. Outside, roosting chickens and tethered goats clucked and bleated, disturbed by the breeze stirring the sandy ground. Rounding a corner we saw Juna up ahead, sitting with his back against a hut, hugging his bent knees. His head was just clear of the window, where candlelight flickered through holes in the rag draped across the cracked pane. We moved back to hide behind a hut, checking to see he was alone.

A sudden gust of wind blew the window open. I listened to the sound of it rattling on loose hinges, watched Juna look up as a hand reached out, pulling it closed.

'Tsk,' Chad let out a low, breathy whistle.

Juna turned and saw us. He paused, one hand pressed against the hut, before coming to us.

I put a hand on his arm and whispered, 'We need you, Juna. Wanda needs you.'

Jaw clenched, he met my eye and nodded. We followed after Chad, back to where the keepers were waiting, and grouped together.

'We need to keep moving,' Chad whispered, distrust in his eye as he looked at Juna. 'Well, are you with us?'

'This way,' Juna said, veering left.

Juna led the way to the edge of the huts, through gardens where mealies grew, past a big old well, and along a track edging the adjoining wall. He stopped at a wooden gate and we regrouped. Then with bows and arrows poised, Chad lifted the latch and led the way through.

On the other side, we found easy cover. We had arrived in what appeared to be a stone forest filled with life-sized statues of animals. Hiding behind an eagle with wings splayed, I looked at the detail of the individual feathers, fingered the intricately carved grooves. There were wolves, lions, deer…; every creature imaginable. This was the epicentre of the King's power, power that had destroyed wildlife, yet the detailed carvings revealed passion for all that had been destroyed. The disparity seemed like madness, until I thought back to what Gogo had said about Rhonad as a young boy; a gifted child who might once have felt the same love for creatures as Wanda did; a boy who had heard Orag speak, turning his gifted mind to insanity.

Whatever the truth of the King, whatever the inspiration for the stone forest, the passion that had once inspired such creations was long gone. A closer look revealed obvious damage: chips in the stonework, great chunks broken off, stone body parts laying discarded on the ground, littered among bottles and kegs. And all watched over by the palace, like a giant beast, old and rotting.

I rubbed my eyes feeling them irritated by grit, and realised the air was slowly filling with sand. Around me the keepers were advancing forward, directed by Juna signalling towards an unassuming doorway. Tasting sand, I pulled my scarf up over my mouth and nose, and followed the others, keeping cover from the narrow lit windows of the palace. Hearing heavy footsteps up ahead, I ducked back behind the stone body of a wolf, and looked out.

Nearby, two figures appeared from around the corner of the palace: a bare-chested man, stumbling as though drunk, with his arm draped over a young girl's shoulders. She appeared just a child, leaning awkwardly beneath the weight of the man twice her size and at least thirty years her senior. Holding a bottle in one hand, with the other he clawed at the girl's dress that was fitted tight around her chest, forcing her immature bosom into a cleavage. I watched him push her roughly against the wall, saw him rip her dress exposing her breasts and pull the skirt up over her waist. Her muffled cries carried on the strengthening winds, ringing in my ears as I tasted wine on my tongue. I reached for my bow, smelling ale and stale sweat in the blustery air. Hearing her cry out when he pressed into her, I pulled back the arrow.

'Suni, no!' I heard Zandi whisper, as I let loose the arrow and watched it hit its target.

There was a moment of silence as the man slumped to the ground, before the girl let out a long shrill scream.

The palace slowly came to life with resounding yells that brought men armed with knives and machetes. I nocked another arrow but with the sandstorm upon us, my eyes were stinging. I pulled the scarf up over my eyes and sank back on my ankles, pushing all thought from my mind as I focused on the abyss. The lights came, and the rushing sense that brought my surroundings into focus. Seeing the men appear as a wall of heat, I side-stepped towards where the keepers were gathering, taking my place in a defensive arch. Arrows were fired, but in the blustery air most failed to hit their target. I watched the men close in, saw flashes of blue from their blades, until we were surrounded. A sudden blow to my head and I stumbled to my knees, blind. As I was dragged across the ground by my feet, I heard the attempts of my comrades to fight back, but with no close range weapons I feared their efforts were futile. My legs were dropped and the scarf pulled down from my eyes. Sheltered from the sandstorm by an overhanging balcony, I saw the keepers dragged out one by one, forced to cower on the ground, captured by the enemy.

Up close, the enemy were not as I'd expected. The town regarded palace guards as disciplined, reputable men, an organised force sworn to protect the King: traits I had seen first-hand at festivals. Juna's account of the mistreatment of palace women was not unexpected, from a regime where men of all ranks exploited women. But these men, on territory that was nothing more than a ruined fortress in the middle of the desert, appeared as disreputable, drunken brutes, worse than the town guards or miners.

They were men of all ages now crowded round us, half dressed, carrying rusty blades in one hand and bottles of ale in the other. They stripped us of our weapons, and tied our hands behind our backs, delivering punches and kicks and a blade to the throat for anyone trying to resist. The stench of ale in the air, the glassy looks in their eyes, warned of violence. Most of all I feared their unpredictability. So far from civilisation of any kind, the thought that we were at their mercy filled me with dread.

One man was looking at me from his one good eye, the other eye withered by a thick scar. He swigged from the bottle and tipped the remainder over my head, then bent down bringing his face close to mine.

'You're witches, from the valley,' he said, revealing blackened teeth. 'You'll tell me why you came here.'

I stared into his eye, teeth clenched. When I didn't answer he grabbed my hair and yanked my head back.

'Hurt her, and I'll kill you,' Zandi said.

He let go of my hair, pushing me sideways as he turned to Zandi. Two men grabbed her arms from behind; the one-eyed man held a knife to her throat as she was forced to her feet. Zandi's eyes shone wild as the tip of the knife pierced her skin, blood streaking her throat.

'We should have a fire tonight,' said one of the men gripping Zandi's arms. 'We'll see how loud witches can scream when they're burning.'

A youth, no more than eighteen years old, bent down in front of Nita, running the point of his knife across her cheek and down her throat. His eyes lingered on her breasts.

'One night with me and I bet I could make you scream,' he said with a smirk.

'I wouldn't touch her if I was you,' another man said. 'Witches have got spells could make your privates fall off.'

'Take them down to the dungeon,' said the one-eyed man. 'A few nights down there and they'll be ready to talk.'

His suggestion seemed to amuse the younger men, who took the lead in jostling us into the palace.

Through the doorway, massive kitchens opened out before us, with the remains of a feast piled high on the centre table. We were led through a narrow arch and down a steep stairwell, guided by a man in-front holding a torch aloft to light the way through the dark dank cellars. Arriving at a barred chamber he unlocked the gate and stood aside, as we were pushed in.

He locked the gate behind us, hooked the torch on the wall and said with a smirk, 'I'll leave you a light; wouldn't want you to miss what you're locked in with.'

Chapter 34

'This is my fault,' I said. 'If I hadn't fired that first arrow...'

'No,' Zandi said, turning to face Juna as she said to him, 'You were the one who led us into this.'

'None of that matters now,' Chad said. 'What matters is finding a way out of here.' He turned to stand back to back with Yuba. 'Give us a hand getting out of these ropes.'

We all paired up, grappling with the ropes. When my hands were freed, I checked the cut on Zandi's neck.

'It's just a scratch,' she said.

'This building looks as rotten as the bastards that live in it,' Chad said, running his hand down the wall, digging his fingers into places where stonework crumbled.

He gripped the bars of the gate and pushed, joined by Yuba, leaning into it with their shoulders, but the gate didn't budge.

'What do you think they meant?' Nita said, looking towards the back of the chamber. 'Locked in with what?'

Juna walked deeper into the chamber and said, 'I think there's something back here.' He put his hand out to touch the wall that rounded a corner. 'It looks like a passage. Maybe there's another way out.'

He led the way down a narrow tunnel that opened out into an adjoining chamber.

'It stinks down here,' Zandi said, covering her nose.

The stench was putrid, like decaying flesh. I looked around the empty chamber, eyes resting on what appeared to be a heap of old rags, like a discarded cape, piled in the corner; until I thought I saw it move.

'What is that?' I said, pointing. 'It just moved.'

'It's probably a rat,' Yuba said.

A strange sound was stirring; soft clicking that formed a buzz and then a hum. It sounded like swarming flies, distant at first but drawing closer. I looked around, confused, since the air was clear aside from the rancid smell. The heap of rags moved again, bulging in places, and slowly, from beneath the pile, something came crawling; fingers and then a human hand. One hand and then another reached out from bony arms, with crusty black sores pitting the flesh. The pile lifted off the ground, revealing two feet with long black toenails like claws. A sickening crack sounded, like bones clicking in the joints, as a head slowly uncurled revealing long straggly hair growing in patches on a scaly scalp. The humming grew louder, like invisible flies swarming about our heads, and a horrifying crack as the head suddenly jerked back, the neck stretched so far back I thought it must be broken. The neck twisted to the side, slowly at first and then with another sudden jerk. I looked in horror as bone pierced the skin, covered in what looked like black blood. Whether a man or a creature, its hand suddenly reached out, grabbing a millipede scaling the wall and dropping it in its mouth.

'What is that?' Nita said, aghast.

At the sound of her voice, the head turned and it scuttled on all fours towards us, accompanied by the same eerie, humming sound. It stopped about a foot away, tilting its head to look up at us with black staring eyes like lifeless marbles. The human-like face was covered in sores so deep I could see bone, and appeared somewhere caught between life and death.

'Who are you?' I asked, horrified and transfixed by the sight of such an unworldly being.

The creature opened its mouth, flicked a long black tongue over cracked lips, and growled, 'Oooooorrraaaaag'.

It kept eyes fixed on us as it crawled backwards, turning away when it reached the wall. I grabbed Zandi's hand and squeezed, watching it scale the vertical surface as easily as a spider, disappearing into a dark crevice.

We retreated back to the first chamber, silent and watchful for the creature following. Even the keepers, non-believers of spirits, couldn't deny what they had witnessed; a foul creature beyond description. Time dragged as we sat with backs pinned against the bars, all eyes fixed in the direction of the passage. Feeling Orag's eyes on us, it was like being trapped in a nightmare we couldn't wake up from, made worse when the torchlight burnt out.

Footsteps sounded from beyond the bars. We shifted round to see, determined to fight back. But as the soft glow of torchlight penetrated the dark, it was a woman's face we saw.

'Juna?' she said, holding the torch out to look among us. 'Are you there?'

'Mother?' Juna said, reaching through the bars.

The woman was so thin she appeared half-starved, a tear collecting in her hollow cheek as she clutched Juna's hand.

'When I heard it was people from the valley, I knew it had to be you,' she said. 'I came as soon as I could. We're getting you out of here.'

'Do you have the keys?' I asked.

'Not yet,' she said. 'But I'll be back with them tomorrow night.'

'They'll kill you,' Juna said.

'They won't know a thing about it till it's too late,' she said. 'I've learnt a few things over the years, like how sleeping potion in your father's ale saves me a beating. All the women are helping. By tomorrow night we'll have enough to drug the kegs.'

'I should never have left you,' Juna said.

'Yes, you should. You just shouldn't have come back.' She let go of his hand and reached for a sack carried over her shoulder, pushing it through the bars. 'Just some bread,' she said. 'It's all I could manage.'

'The men could come back for us before tomorrow night,' Zandi said.

'They won't,' Juna's mother said. 'They plan on keeping you down here for at least a week.'

'What about that thing we're locked in with,' Nita said. 'It calls itself, Orag.'

'It might call itself that,' Juna's mother said, 'but it's still a man, and harmless from what I can tell. It doesn't come out of its hole.'

'It looks half dead,' I said. 'Who is it?'

'He used to call himself Rhonad,' she said. 'But I don't know if he even remembers that name anymore.'

'Rhonad?' I said. 'You mean the King? That's impossible.'

'He's been down here for years,' she said.

'I don't understand,' I said. 'That thing in there can't be Rhonad. I saw the King only a few years ago at the festival in town; he was still a young man.'

'You only saw what they wanted you to see,' she said. 'This palace is built on lies; for long enough, not even the women here knew the truth. I found their secret out about ten years ago, when they locked me down here for 'stealing' food.'

I stared at her aghast but she appeared completely sincere. Despite all that my mother had known, and believed, even she had never doubted that it was Rhonad at the festivals.

'It's unbelievable,' I said. 'The whole town, none of them, have any idea. They think the King is all powerful, protected by the Orag's enchantment.'

'The enchantment is all the lies the men tell,' she said. 'The spirit of Orag is powerful, just not in ways they claim. It has the power to possess a man; you've seen for yourself what Rhonad has become. Years ago his own men became afraid of him. They hatched a plan to lock him down here; he's been left to rot ever since.'

'But why?' I said.

'The men here own the crystals,' she said. 'They're wealthy and answerable to no one. They keep wives and children as their slaves, spend their days intoxicated by liquor, and enjoy the company of girls, kidnapped or sold. They're ruinous, and getting more rotten with each generation. And they're dominant, power they'd tell any number of lies to hold onto.'

'But who did I see at the festival?' I asked.

'Just a young man,' she said. 'They send a man to the festival, hide his face behind a shroud and tell stories of a powerful King who never grows old. Whether it's because they're feared, or because they include elements of the truth, they get away with it.'

'My father,' Juna said. 'He knew about this?'

She nodded and said, 'Your father's as rotten as the rest, you know that.' She reached through the bars to touch his cheek. 'Why did you come back? Why did any of you come here?'

She listened, eyes shining, as we told of our quest.

Chapter 35

As promised, Juna's mother returned the following day carrying a ring of keys. She fumbled as she tried each key in turn, dropping them in her haste; they fell, clanging loudly against the metal bars. She reached down to pick them up, pausing as she straightened to stand. Hearing the eerie clicking hum, smelling the putrid odour, I turned and saw Rhonad emerge from the passageway. He was standing upright, his head bent low, long straggly hair hanging down over his face, his body jerking from side to side as he shuffled towards us. We parted as he came through, appalled by the thought of his touch. Juna's mother tried another key and this time it turned. She pulled the gate open and stepped aside, forced to let Rhonad walk free. We watched him disappear into the cellars beyond, listening to the eerie hum fade.

'Come on,' Juna's mother said, ushering us out. 'Find what you're looking for and get out of here.'

We emerged from the cellars, into the kitchen, where a group of women were gathered around the table. There was fear etched on their gaunt faces, as they clutched one another. Like Juna's mother, they were skeletal; their work-hardened skin and chapped hands signs of lives of labour.

'Come, eat,' Juna's mother said, pushing plates of bread and meat towards us.

'Sunette,' one woman said. 'You let Rhonad out!'

'I had no choice,' Sunette said. 'Which way did he go?'

All the women looked towards a wide arch on the far side of the kitchen.

Sunette held her hand out to a young girl; her hairstyle and revealing dress reminded me of life in the brothel. She appeared more frightened than anyone, as she walked towards Sunette and took her hand.

'Tell them,' Sunette said to the girl.

'What you're looking for,' the girl said to us, 'the lion's head. I've heard the men speak about it. I think it's in the royal bed chamber.'

'Where's that?' I asked.

'Upstairs,' she said. 'I don't know where, but I don't think it's in the south wing.'

'We collected your weapons,' Sunette said, gesturing to them, piled in the corner. 'We laced the ale, but have them ready just in case.'

We left the women in the kitchen and filed through the archway into a huge entrance hall, with a wide staircase leading up to an overlooking balcony. Hallways branched from all four corners, the walls filled with antlers, tusks and skulls. Seeing two men slumped against the main doors as though unconscious, Yuba went and kicked them but they didn't stir. We climbed the staircase, seeing the upstairs had the same design; four hallways leading to four separate wings. Split into groups to search, I followed Juna into the west wing.

Passageways branched left and right, the walls all littered with dusty bones. Men slept where they had fallen, while girls watched with frightened eyes as we stole on by. All the rooms were finely furnished, with silk sheets on the beds, fine drapes at the windows, and upholstered furnishings. In one room we saw men slumped around a table, a big bowl in the centre overflowing with crystals. We kept going, checking each room, seeing mounted antlers and skulls, but there was no sign of a lion's skull.

'We've been down here already,' Juna said, looking up at a skull with tusks like a boar. 'This place is a maze.'

'Sshh,' Zandi hissed from behind. 'Listen.'

The eerie humming sound, distant at first, was drawing closer. Rhonad appeared further down the hallway, shuffling out of one corridor and disappearing down another.

'It's his old chamber we're looking for,' I said. 'He might lead us to it.'

We followed from a distance, halting when we rounded a corner that lead to a dead end. Rhonad was shuffling towards a door bolted from the outside. He stopped in front of it and cocked his head. Abruptly, he raised his arms in the air, bones cracking, before he brought his fists crashing down against the door. Wood splintered beneath the blows until the entire door was left swinging on one hinge, and Rhonad's arms hung at his sides, bent and broken, black blood oozing where a spike of wood pierced one wrist. Oblivious, he looked straight ahead and shuffled into the room.

We crept after him, and peered through the doorway. The eerie humming sounded all around him, accompanied by a beastly growling that sounded to be coming from Rhonad. He was shuffling around the room, pausing every so often, head cocked, looking at the window, the drapes, the wardrobe… He stopped with his back to us, at the foot of a four poster bed, staring towards the headboard; above it, hanging on the wall, was a dusty old skull with opened jaws and long fangs.

'That must be it,' Zandi whispered.

Rhonad's head turned as he growled, 'It's mine.'

We watched in horror as his neck twisted so far round, that even with his back to us, he glared straight at us. His head flinched from side to side, blackened teeth gnashing, as slowly his head tilted backwards, his mouth dropping open until it was gaping wide. Then an unworldly scream rose out of his mouth, sounding with two contrasting pitches, high and low. The long continuous scream brought a black substance, like thick pulp, bubbling up from his mouth. It foamed and coiled in one long stream reaching up towards the ceiling, still attached to Rhonad when it burst into flame. Fire swept down the black pulp, over Rhonad's face and down the length of his body. Engulfed in flame, his arms splayed at his sides as he rose from the ground to hang mid-air.

A gust of wind seemed to come from nowhere. Rhonad, burning, flew back onto the bed, setting the sheets alight. Juna ran into the room, around the bed, and reached up for the skull. The fire rose, a ball of orange billowing across the ceiling, devouring everything.

'Juna!' I yelled.

Fire was sweeping across the walls as he ran back with the skull. A stone lintel cracked, bringing the ceiling crashing down, as we fled.

All through the halls the fire spread. Girls came running from all directions, coughing and spluttering from smoke and dust as the palace burned. Down the staircase and through the kitchens, stone imploded in fire behind us. We gathered outside on the edge of the stone forest, keepers, wives, children and mistresses, all watching the palace burn to rubble.

'Father!' a boy came screaming. A woman grabbed him but he pulled away, running towards the burning palace. Chad caught hold of his arm, pulling him back while the boy kicked and screamed, 'Witches! You killed my father!'

As children cried and girls clung to one another in confusion, the palace wives watched with silent calm.

'How did this happen?' Sunette asked, clutching Juna's shoulders.

'It was Rhonad,' Juna said. 'He – he burst into fire. He's dead.'

Zandi put her arm around me and said, 'It's over.'

I looked at the smouldering rubble, watched the cloud of dust and ash billow up into the sky; a giant plume of smoky grey. But among the natural tones a dark patch gathered, moving independently of the swirling cloud, making its way to the edge. It broke free, a black, man-sized mass drifting away against the southerly breeze.

'The dead can't die,' I said, fearing the prophecy was in motion. 'We need to get back to the forest.'

Zandi went with the keepers to gather the horses, while I waited with Juna, sensing he was torn.

'Come with us,' he said to his mother.

She smiled, shook her head and said, 'My place is with the women. We've been silenced for so long, but the town needs to hear the truth, and we need to tell it. The Mantra's return is for all of us.' She held his face in her hands, lowered his head and kissed him on the forehead.

'I'm so proud of you, Juna. So many boys here turn out like their fathers, but not you.'

'I have you to thank for everything,' Juna said.

'No,' she said. 'You found your own way. One day I'll see this valley of yours. Now go. And don't look back, not to here.'

Sunette's courage, the courage of all the women, brought hope for the town that had once cast me out.

The skull was carefully wrapped in cloth, and placed in a large wood box for the journey. True to his mother's word, Juna kept his eye on the journey ahead. But I did look back, as a convoy of camels headed away, carrying women and children west towards the town. So much was set to change, more than I could ever have imagined. How would the town react? Once there had been only a persecuted few, soon the palace women would stand against the lies. I wondered that others might step out from the shadows and do the same.

Chapter 36

I didn't speak of my fear that Orag had risen from the charred hull of the palace. Journeying across the desert I glimpsed the same entity in the skies ahead of our path; a wayward black cloud drifting against the breeze. With a pace faster than our convoy, it drifted from sight, heading in the direction of the mountains. I imagined it as a detached limb, searching for its origin. Others didn't see it, or perhaps chose not to. We had witnessed horrors not easily forgotten; our only goal was to return home, and lay the lion skull to rest.

Reaching the mountains, we dismounted and led the horses in single file up a steep ascent.

'Watch out up there,' Bindi shouted out from the back, side-stepping a cascade of shale.

'It's not us,' Yuba shouted down from the front.

'We must get off this slope,' Zandi called.

All around, patches of loose stone were shifting. I looked up beyond our convoy, seeing a slow wave of shale coming towards us from higher up the slope.

'This way,' Yuba shouted back, veering right towards a bulging cliff face.

Traversing the path in the shadow of the cliff, I heard a splintering sound. I looked up and saw a crack form in the cliff, snaking its way down through the rock.

'Hurry!' I shouted, feeling the ground rumble beneath my feet.

Giant shards of rock broke free of the cliff, tumbling down the mountainside behind us. Keepers grabbed horses that were bucking. I looked back at the rolling boulders generating landslides, held out my arms to steady myself as the earth shook, anxious about the enormous power of Orag shaking apart the very mountains.

On the other side of a deep ravine, the mountainside appeared stable. We made for a narrow ledge skirting the vast walls, leaning into the solid slope as we coaxed the frightened horses along. Midway along the path, a dust cloud rained down on us; the fine particles were soon replaced by rocks. Pinned against the wall, the peaks crumbling onto us, a spiked fragment broke free, shattering through the ledge just behind me. I looked back at Bindi, the last of our convoy, trapped on the other side of the gap, clinging onto the mane of a horse that was rearing.

Time slowed into confusing sights and sounds: stones tumbling onto my head, blood oozing down my check; Nita's scream piercing the air as the ledge beneath Bindi's feet gave way; Zandi gripping my shoulders, pulling me back. I stared, transfixed by the silent horror on Bindi's face as she suddenly vanished. The screams of the horse drowned out all else as I watched them plummet into the ravine.

Zandi pulled me to her just as another massive rock sliced through the ledge I had been standing on. We drove the horses on, out of the ravine, arriving at the escarpment on the other side, our faces masks of terror and despair. The loss of Bindi cut through us. Grief distorted Nita's face. But mountains showed no mercy: the rumbling ground drove us on as we fled across the escarpment.

Terror reigned behind our heels as we made a frantic bid to reach safe ground. But no-where was safe, as though our own footsteps triggered the mountain's wrath. We ran beyond exhaustion, beyond despair, energised only by the wild instinct to survive, the movement of the sun tracing our desperate journey west, as we slowly gained ground on the summits. Finally, realising the shuddering ground had stilled, I paused to rest. I looked ahead at Zandi, Nita leaning heavily against her, and the line of keepers trailing further up the path. Beyond them, peeking from behind the flat-topped summit, two tall peaks rose high in the sky.

'Come on,' Juna said, coming up behind me. 'We should keep moving.'

'I think we're over the mines,' I said, nervously anticipating an end to the calm.

Our eyes locked as we heard a deep groan rise up from below ground. He grabbed my hand and pulled me on, clear of a gaping crack that split the ground. Another moment of calm before the ground behind us suddenly dropped, leaving a giant crater.

Everyone ran for higher ground, as giant sinkholes patched the slopes. In the chaos of rock-fall and our own yells, I heard what sounded like muffled screams and thought of boys trapped underground. Veering left over a bulging rock face, I paused to look down over a lone tower surrounded by rubble; it was all that was left of the entrance to the mines. This was now a vast gravesite, until I saw movement in amongst the rubble as survivors managed to claw their way free from the network of underground chambers. Feeling the earth tremor, I slowly raised my gaze towards the flattened summit; *Ntombi.*

I ran on past the keepers, hearing Juna and Zandi yell out my name as I clawed my way over the topmost ledge. The roof of the brothel, once solid rock, had collapsed into a giant crater, with the dusty bodies of girls crawling out. I looked frantically at survivors, but Ntombi was not among their frightened faces.

'Suni!' Juna and Zandi called, as I climbed down towards the centre of the crater that disappeared into a hole. 'What are you doing? Get out of there.'

'I have to find her,' I shouted back. 'I have to find Ntombi.'

I sat down in the dirt, pushing forwards to slide into the dark hole. When the ground levelled out, I felt around in the dusty surrounds, at what felt to be a table leg, and smashed crockery.

'Ntombi!' I called, but there was no reply.

'Stay where you are,' Zandi's voice called down from above. 'We're coming down.'

They landed close by, two dusty faces just visible in the narrow shaft of light. On hands and knees we crawled through the rubble, calling Ntombi's name.

'I've found someone,' Zandi finally said.

Following the sound of her voice, I found her crouched beside a pile of rubble, where Ntombi looked out, buried beneath the stone.

'Ntombi, I'm here,' I said, leaning over to look in her eyes. 'We're going to get you out.'

I can't feel my legs,' she said, her voice weak, her eyes screwed as though in pain. 'Where's my baby?'

I put a hand on her brow and said, 'Baby?'

'There's someone else here,' Juna said.

'My baby?' Ntombi whispered.

I left Zandi carefully clearing stones piled on top of Ntombi, and found Juna kneeling beside a body. It was Wiseman, eyes closed, mouth gaping, dead.

'You've got to get Ntombi out of here,' I said to Juna. 'I'll look for the child.'

I crawled around, sweeping my hands along the ground, listening for a murmur, a cry, anything, but found no signs of a baby. Hearing a distant groan rise up from the ground, I scrambled backwards.

'Suni!' Zandi called. 'Come on, get out of there.'

A sudden burst of flame broke through the rubble, spurting a shower of hot dust. The fire was sucked back down as suddenly as it had appeared, and in its place came a baby's heart-wrenching cries.

'Luna!' Ntombi screamed.

I found the child wrapped in a blanket, seemingly unscathed from the fire. I picked her up and carried her out of the hole, returning her to her mother. By the light of the moon I saw Ntombi's legs were crushed, covered in blood, and across the baby's cheek, a flaring red burn. They were injured, but alive.

Chapter 37

The valley beyond the mountains was calm. Only our dusty faces and anguished expressions, as we rode hard over the plains, revealed a prophecy in motion.

Arriving at the forest, the villagers received us with a chorus of joyous, high-pitched wailing, as though oblivious to our exhaustion. At the graveside the elders kept a respectful silence, though their eyes shone with anticipation when I rested the box with the lion's skull beside the grave. Only Gogo remained sombre throughout, kneeling with hands gently clasped in her lap, Wanda on one side of her, her mysterious stones scattered on the other. Looking into her watery eyes, I wondered if she had seen all we had survived. She said nothing, just closed her eyes and breathed in deeply as the cries of Bindi's mother filled the forest.

Juna carried Ntombi and her child over to where Wanda lay. I told Ntombi all about Wanda's gift, and of his remarkable journey. I anticipated her being concerned for her nephew, and proud of how special he was. Holding Luna in one arm, she reached out, her hand hovering over Wanda's face. I thought she would touch him but she withdrew her hand. Her gaze lingered but her eyes gave nothing away, before she turned her attention back to Luna. Seeing her with Luna was a side of Ntombi I had not seen before, maternal instincts she'd never shown for Wanda. I watched her leave, carried to Sisi's hut; a healer experienced in mending bones.

I sat beside Wanda and held his hand, as villagers carefully dug into the grave. Seeing animal remains and the care taken in uncovering them brought tears to my eyes. I thought of the palace, all the bones shamefully hung on the walls; I could only hope the fire had brought some peace to the dead. When Juna handed the skull to Gogo, she carefully unwrapped it while whispering words I couldn't hear. Elders circling the grave joined hands, gently swaying from side to side as they joined Gogo in a low-pitched, melodic chant:

'*Sarayon, sarayon, taroah, a manantu a Mantra. Sarayon, sarayon, taroah, funiswa oh shahim. Sarayon, sarayon, taroah, a manantu a Mantra.*'

Villagers played a sombre rhythm on the drums, and my heart beat in time. As the pounding grew louder and faster, the elders waved their hands in the air, their voices echoing through the trees. Gogo picked up the lion's skull in both hands and held it out over the grave. A breeze stirred through the trees, gentle at first but growing stronger, sounding with a resounding 'hush'. Gogo lowered the skull onto the edge of the grave and released it. As it rolled into the dug-out earth, the breeze picked up into a gust, swirling in circles around us. Earth and bones moved around the skull, as it slowly sank into the ground. When completely covered in its final resting place, the air fell still.

I looked from the grave into the trees, feeling the mystery of the occasion, wondering whether the Mantra was close. But nothing looked back. I looked across the faces of elders and villagers, seeing their eyes shining wet with tears, and finally rested my gaze on Wanda. As the drumbeats slowed to a gentle stop, Wanda's eyes opened.

'Welcome back,' I said.

He gazed deep into my eyes, with an intense look that seemed to see through me. In that moment he was like a stranger. He didn't speak as I carried him to Sisi's hut, but just stared out towards the trees.

There was an awkward reunion, Ntombi and Wanda quietly regarding each other from across the room. But when Juna stepped forward to help bandage Ntombi's legs, Wanda moved in closer. He stopped some distance from the bed and I moved in behind him. Remembering Ntombi's behaviour towards him the last time they had seen one another, I put a reassuring hand on Wanda's shoulder. Ntombi saw the gesture and looked at me, eyes gently narrowed; I wondered if she felt regret. She looked down at Wanda, the corners of her mouth slowly turning up into a nervous smile.

'Hello Wanda,' Ntombi finally said.

After a moment of silence, Wanda replied, 'Hello.'

Ntombi looked from him to me, eyebrows raised, as slowly she reached out for his hand.

I stayed a while, watching Juna tend the bonds between three wounded souls; he would nurture them like birds fallen from the nest.

As the days passed I saw Ntombi and Juna's gaze linger. It was a thought that made me smile, knowing that in Juna, Ntombi would find someone kind and dependable. If anyone could heal the rifts of this fragile family, I knew Juna could. Weeks passed and he never left Ntombi's side, as Ntombi recovered in Sisi's hut with Luna.

Zandi and I spent the days with Wanda, roaming the forest where new life was stirring. Fruit trees, long barren, began to blossom, bringing the return of fruit bats and monkeys with curious yellow noses. Each evening we returned to the hut to tell Juna of all we had seen. He put names to our sightings of species long thought extinct.

The forest was changing. So too were its people. Through Rhonad, the keepers had seen the face of Orag, had sacrificed one of their own; Bindi was lost but would never be forgotten. Once sceptical of the elders' beliefs, now the keepers looked upon Gogo's stones with an open mind, as she told that the breaking was over, the Mantra had returned. And so we watched and waited for a sighting of our Great Spirit, but none came.

Ntombi's legs healed enough to free her of pain, though she would never walk again. Still, with Juna at her side, and Luna nestled at her breast, she appeared content. As the weeks passed, love and friendship grew between Juna and Ntombi, until the day came when they declared their intention to marry.

It was a simple ceremony, held in the village. Gogo said the blessings as they swapped garlands of flowers, tying them in matrimony. Wanda stood at Juna's side, while Ntombi held Luna, looking radiant as seeds were thrown over their heads. I waved as they set off in a mule and cart for Juna's cottage, promising to visit soon.

'You're supposed to be happy,' Zandi said, handing me a handkerchief. I wiped my eyes and wrapped an arm around her waist. 'Come on,' she said. 'Let's go home.' I smiled to think of our crude treehouse as home.

Lying with Zandi at night, together we experienced the true meaning of intimacy. Feeling the closeness of the bond we shared, I knew I had found someone I could not bear to be parted from, yet I was torn. In the afternoons I would visit Gogo and ask her to look into the stones. She spoke of the eye of Orag having turned from us, a reassuring response but not the answer I sought.

One day she turned to me and said, 'Suni, I don't need to look at the stones to see what's in your heart. You'll be leaving us.'

Until she said the words I had doubted I would. But her gaze was penetrating, stirring longings I had kept buried. The town had been Mata's home, my home, and now the palace wives were there delivering the truth to a people kept in ignorance. They had torn me from my mother, had cast me out; an injustice that still remained. I feared I would never be able to find true peace, until I saw those same people acknowledge their wrongs. Moreover, quite simply, I realised I missed the streets of home.

I returned to the treehouse, to find Zandi sitting with legs dangling over the broad bough. She watched as I climbed the rope ladder to join her, stared, one eyebrow raised, as I sat down next to her.

'What?' I said, unnerved by the intensity on her face.

'You tell me,' she said.

I smiled and shrugged, turning away to look into the trees.

'I may not have Gogo's stones,' she said, 'but you're really not that hard to read. You want to leave.'

I shook my head and said, 'I would never leave you. I've been thinking about my hometown, that's all, but here, with you, is my home now.'

She linked her arm through mine and said, 'You need to go back. After everything that's happened, I don't think you'll rest until you do.' She nudged me and said, 'Don't look so worried; I'm coming with you.'

I looked at her, eyebrows raised, and said, 'You'd do that?'

She smiled and said, 'I want to see where you come from; I want to see the town and the river and the ocean. And if it doesn't work out, we can always come back to the forest.'

'You'll always have a home here,' Gogo said, as I said goodbye to her the next morning.

It was a reassuring thought as I faced an unknown journey. The townspeople of Shendi had long been my enemies, and even now I had no idea what to expect. But in this distant valley I had kin; a sanctuary I could always return to.

I had left my hometown a sixteen-year-old girl, afraid and unprepared as the skies had come crashing down around me. Some five years on, I was returning a young woman no longer afraid and overwhelmed. The world had proven to be bigger than I could have imagined, but I had not been alone in overcoming the many trials I had faced. And now, Zandi was with me.

Riding with Zandi east up the embankment, we stopped for a final look at the forest, heartened by the sight of tree saplings sprouting beyond the boundary. But there was something else, a flash of colour, movement in the canopy. At the forest edge the treetops parted and a head appeared, reaching high on a long, maned neck. The mystical creature gave only a fleeting appearance before it turned to head back into the trees, and as it did, its face transformed from monkey to deer to wolf to bird.

'The Mantra has returned,' I said to Wanda, sitting next to him on the front step of the cottage, the owl perched on his shoulder.

He looked at me, head cocked, and smiled; it was an expression too old for his years.

'You did it,' he said.

'No, Wanda, you did it.' I put an arm around him as we gazed out at a passing herd of deer. 'I'm going to miss you.'

I had taken him with me once, but not this time. The valley was his home, and surrounded by wolves and bats and deer and birds, it was the rightful place for a boy with a gift. The Mantra had returned to breathe life into our homeland, and with it I felt hope.

Other novels, novellas and short story collections available from Stairwell Books

Carol's Christmas	N.E. David
Feria	N.E. David
A Day at the Races	N.E. David
Running With Butterflies	John Walford
Foul Play	P J Quinn
Poison Pen	P J Quinn
Wine Dark, Sea Blue	A.L. Michael
Skydive	Andrew Brown
Close Disharmony	P J Quinn
When the Crow Cries	Maxine Ridge
The Geology of Desire	Clint Wastling
Homelands	Shaunna Harper
Border 7	Pauline Kirk
Tales from a Prairie Journal	Rita Jerram
Here in the Cull Valley	John Wheatcroft
How to be a Man	Alan Smith
A Multitude of Things	David Clegg
Know Thyself	Lance Clarke
Thinking of You Always	Lewis Hill
Rapeseed	Alwyn Marriage
A Shadow in My Life	Rita Jerram
Tyrants Rex	Clint Wastling
Abernathy	Claire Patel-Campbell
The Go-to Guy	Neal Hardin

For further information please contact rose@stairwellbooks.com

www.stairwellbooks.co.uk
@stairwellbooks